CHRISTMAS
IN MY HEART

14

FOCUS ON THE FAMILY®

# CHRISTMAS IN MY HEART

## A TREASURY OF TIMELESS CHRISTMAS STORIES

14

*compiled and edited by*

JOE L. WHEELER



TYNDALE HOUSE PUBLISHERS, INC., WHEATON, ILLINOIS

Visit Tyndale's exciting Web site at www.tyndale.com and the author's at www.joewheelerbooks.com

*TYNDALE* is a registered trademark of Tyndale House Publishers, Inc.

Tyndale's quill logo is a trademark of Tyndale House Publishers, Inc.

*Focus on the Family* is a registered trademark of Focus on the Family, Colorado Springs, Colorado.

*Christmas in My Heart* is a registered trademark of Joe L. Wheeler and may not be used by anyone else in any form.

*Christmas in My Heart 14*



Woodcut illustrations are from the library of Joe L. Wheeler.

Designed by Alyssa Force

Series designed by Jenny Swanson

Edited by Kimberly Miller

Published in association with WordServe Literary Group, Ltd., 10152 Knoll Circle, Highlands Ranch, CO 80130.

---

**Library of Congress Cataloging-in-Publication Data**

Christmas in my heart / [compiled by] Joe L. Wheeler.
p. cm.
ISBN 978-1-4143-0135-8 (14)
ISBN 1-4143-0135-9 (14)
1. Christmas stories, American. I. Wheeler, Joe L., date
PS648.C45C447 1992
813′.01833—dc20

---

Printed in the United States of America

10 09 08 07 06 05
7 6 5 4 3 2 1

# DEDICATION

Of the time that is not spent researching or writing,
much of it is spent doing media interviews.
Reason being: it doesn't do much good
to create books if no one buys them.

Over the years, I've had many interview-bookers;
some have been quite good at what they do,
some *very* good, and a precious few *superlatively* good.
Of the latter group, there is one person who,
for several months each year, appears to live in
our house, as she is either phoning, e-mailing,
or faxing us about a new interview or rescheduling
one already on the books. She continually cracks
the whip—but gently, and always with a smile in her
voice. In fact, her voice *always* has joy bells in it!

So it gives me great pleasure to dedicate
*Christmas in My Heart 14* to someone who
is unexcelled at what she does, a true
wonder-worker who is loved and admired
by all who know her:

JILL SWANSON

of

Tyndale House Publishers, Inc.

# CONTENTS

## ACKNOWLEDGMENTS

"Time to Stand Up," (Introduction) by Joseph Leininger Wheeler. Copyright © 2004. Printed by permission of the author.

"The Christmas Wish," by Arthur Gordon. Published in *Guideposts Christmas Treasury*, 1972. Reprinted by permission of Pamela Gordon.

"A Tree for Benji," by Harold Ivan Smith. Reprinted with permission from *Charisma & Christian Life*, December 1951. Copyright © Strang Communications. All rights reserved. www.charismamag.com.

"Sea Anchor," by Marjorie Yourd Hill. If anyone can provide knowledge of earliest publication source of this old story, or the whereabouts of the author or the author's next of kin, please send to Joe Wheeler (P.O. Box 1246, Conifer, Colorado 80433).

"The Soft Spot in B606," author unknown. If anyone can provide knowledge of the author or author's next of kin of this very old story, please send to Joe Wheeler (P.O. Box 1246, Conifer, Colorado 80433).

"The Night My Father Came Home," author unknown. If anyone can provide knowledge of the author or author's next of kin, of this old story, please send to Joe Wheeler (P.O. Box 1246, Conifer, Colorado 80433).

"How Dot Heard *The Messiah*," by Hezekiah Butterworth. Published in *Wide Awake*, December 1881.

"A Certain Star," by Pearl S. Buck. Reprinted by permission of Harold Ober Associates, Incorporated. © 1957 by Pearl S. Buck. Copyright renewed 1985.

"Season of Uncertainty," by Nancy N. Rue. Published in *Breakaway*, December 1996. Reprinted by permission of the author.

"The Miracle of Christmas," by Earl Reed Silvers. Published in *Young People's Weekly*, December 23, 1933. Text reprinted by permission of Joe Wheeler (P.O. Box 1246, Conifer, Colorado 80433) and Cook Communications Ministries, Colorado Springs, Colorado.

"The Gift that Never Was," by Lanita Kampton. Copyright © 1997. Printed by permission of the author.

"A Boy Named John," author unknown. If anyone can provide knowledge of the author or author's next of kin, of this old story, please send to Joe Wheeler (P.O. Box 1246, Conifer, Colorado 80433).

"The Christmas Gift," by Dorothy Boys Kilian. Published in *The Christian Home*, December 1958 (The Graded Press, Nashville, Tennessee). Reprinted by permission of Abingdon Press, Nashville, Tennessee. If anyone knows the whereabouts of the author or author's next of kin, please send to Joe Wheeler (P.O. Box 1246, Conifer, Colorado 80433).

"There's a Song in the Air," by Katherine Reeves. Published in *The Christian Home,* December 1958 (The Graded Press, Nashville, Tennessee). Reprinted by permission of Abingdon Press, Nashville, Tennessee. If anyone knows the whereabouts of the author or author's next of kin, please send to Joe Wheeler (P.O. Box 1246, Conifer, Colorado 80433).

"By the Fireplace," by Joseph Leininger Wheeler. Copyright © 2004. Reprinted by permission of the author.

❄ ❄ ❄

*Joseph Leininger Wheeler*

# INTRODUCTION: TIME TO STAND UP

---

*Think back to the last time you were part of a large crowd at a public gathering and felt convicted that you should stand up and express your feelings on a certain matter. Do you remember how your hands got clammy, how your temperature climbed, how you worried,* What if they don't like what I say? Will they think I'm a dummy?

*Then, if you did stand up, do you remember how your voice shook, how you could not find a place for your hands, and how you felt afterward when someone told you, "My! I'm glad you spoke out! I feel the same way, but was too chicken to stand up." Amazingly, more and more people today feel compelled to take such a stand for Christmas.*

Not long ago, I heard a story about a gentleman who lives in a midsized community in one of our Western states. Last year, while attending a meeting of his town's chamber of commerce, the leader of that town's annual Christmas parade proposed to the group that they change this event's name to "Holiday Parade."

He was so persuasive, telling them that this was the "in thing" to do, that the motion passed. But this one attendee with guts stood up and said, "Most of the chamber members aren't here today. I think we need to get a broader consensus on this before we change the name." The proposer/persuader was stunned, for he didn't dream anyone would oppose him! Afterward, the attendee-with-guts contacted all the ministers in the area and asked each one to take the matter to their respective congregation and report their conclusions back to the chamber. You guessed it! When they did so, demanding with one voice that "Christmas Parade" be left unchanged, the chamber members quickly reversed their earlier vote.

Every time we are convicted to stand up, to speak out, but do nothing, not only is our cause weakened, but so are we: next time we will be even more unlikely to speak out when we are convicted to do so.

Well, it's time for us to stand up for Christmas. Not long after that chamber reversed its decision on the Christmas parade, newly elected Mayor Hickenlooper of the city of Denver announced that, in 2005, "Happy Holidays" would replace the words "Merry Christmas" in lights on city headquarters. Had that been all, the issue might have died right there, but only a couple of days later, citizens learned that the organizer of Denver's annual Parade of Lights had informed an area minister that his church could not sing Christmas carols in the parade (separation of church and state, you know). That did it: the national media jumped in, church leaders spoke out, individual voters spoke out, and the next thing we knew, a somewhat chastened mayor spoke out and deadpanned, "'Hickenlooper' might have two o's, but I am not 'Scrooge,'" and declared that "Merry Christmas" would stay.

Taken singly, none of these three stories might appear to be very significant, but taken together they are very significant indeed. Permit me to explain why.

America was born a predominantly Christian nation. Though the Founding Fathers advocated separation of church and state, that didn't mean that they disenfranchised God! God was incorporated into every swearing in of our leaders, every presidential inauguration, every court affirmation of truth: "So help me, God." God's name was said with respect in virtually every civic or government gathering, inscribed into the fresco and walls of the government buildings themselves, and even inscribed on our legal tender ("In God we trust"). Even the U.S. Senate had its chaplain—it still has one today! And every session opens with prayer.

That continued to be true for over two hundred years. Our national and local leaders continued to be men and women of faith. Then things began to change: slowly at first, then with increasing speed. First, cinema. Conservative at first, and then, reflecting Mae West's immortal quip: "I used to be Snow White—but I drifted," cinema began to drift. Television didn't really make its presence known until right after World War II: it too started out conservatively, strongly emphasizing traditional family values. Within a decade, here, too, a drift occurred. By the sixties, TV began to turn dark, and each decade since, the level of acceptable behavior, language, subject matter, and imagery has gone further south. None of the channels even pretends to offer family hour programming anymore. And now cable TV comes along with virtually no controls at all. The same is true for the Internet. It is a terrifying world in which to raise a child.

Before writing my 1993 book on the impact of TV on the American home, *Remote Controlled*, I researched the subject for thirty years. What I found strangely inexplicable were the muted responses from ostensibly Christian parents to the gradual blueing of the media, the descent from one-time decency to every perversion and taboo imaginable. Public outcry to even pedophilia was almost nonexistent. Neither did people speak out when it became the accepted thing to mock traditional family and Christian values—not just mocking but portraying those who attempt to live by these values as buffoons or extremists. No wonder America's media has taken our supineness as carte blanche to continue producing more of the same.

No wonder other nations call America "the Great Satan." And they wonder, *Yet they claim to be a Christian nation!*

We've gone even further in our refusal to take a stand. I know plenty of Christians who regularly take their families to R-rated movies, rationalizing, *Well, everybody else is doing it: they're going to make these movies anyhow—what difference could we make, after all?* What difference? Every time one of us buys a ticket for a smutty film, with every third word being either sacrilegious or obscene, we might just as well be telling the producers: *Keep it up! Give us more of the same!* There is an old saying that is apropos here: "Evil triumphs when good people do nothing."

During the last decade of the old millennium, thousands of parents began taking a long, hard look at what was being fed into the hearts, minds, and souls of their children. After doing so, they concluded that they had no choice: either they were going to see their children destroyed by the media juggernaut (cinema, radio, TV, MTV, video, DVD, Internet, soft-porn print, and other forms of intrusion) or they were going to have to make family the number-one priority of their life and curtail media intrusion into their home. Many went even further and began homeschooling their children at the cost of considerable creature comforts.

I believe that nothing short of an American revolution is really going to turn things around. It is not enough just to homeschool; it is not enough to take control of the avenues to our children's minds, hearts, and souls such as cutting down on some of the million commercials each twenty-year-old will have seen in their lifetime (very few of them being compatible with the values we profess to live by). No, none of this is enough.

It is long past time for every last person in Western society to realize that God holds us accountable for our witness. He expects *each* of us to make a daily difference. And there is no such thing as a "small thing" in life. The most powerful sermons our children will ever hear will not be heard in churches, synagogues, cathedrals, mosques, or temples—but rather they will be *heard* at home. Children are impacted, not so much by what we claim to profess, but rather by what we *do*. They not only hear our words, but they also catch the tone and watch the body language. And they most certainly will not buy into what we fail to do ourselves.

It is also long past time for us to stop being sidetracked by numbers. What can one individual do? Well, Christ turned the world upside down with only twelve. What can one family do? That one family can change an entire community. What can one church do? Well, each church spire represents a gathering of people who profess to be living by godly values. What if our church congregations began weighing in on issues by speaking out individually as well as collectively; by writing letters to newspaper editors and media magnates and registering their commitment to decency and honoring those who try to live by moral values (those values being shared by virtually every civilization on earth)? For parents in most any part of the world agree on one thing: they want their children to grow up to be kind, generous, honest, faithful, industrious, affable, respectful to elders, astute, helpful, and clean living. What if individuals, families, and churches began boycotting networks and advertisers that failed to offer programming that was positive, uplifting, inspirational, and clean? What if they did the same with movies? If two Christmas movies, for example, come out, one compatible with Christianity and another saturated with subtle put-downs of spiritual things, we could make our voices heard by attending only the one that upholds a Christ-centered Christmas.

Look what happened when millions of concerned citizens showed up to vote last November. The U.S. election of 2004 ended up being a referendum on values. And, wonder of wonders, millions ended up taking a stand for those values. It was fascinating to see newscasters and talk show hosts struggling to regain their erstwhile cocksureness. For so long it had been popular to trash religion and those who practiced it—unless it was Eastern or New Age—that they just couldn't cope with looking at the election demographics and realizing that they were in such a minority in their antireligion and anti–Judeo-Christian stance. (As time has passed, however, they have already begun to rationalize away the significance of the election results.)

Don't get me wrong: I don't mean by all this that we should become dictatorial, saying, in effect: *There are X-million voting church members out there, more than there are of you! If you don't do as we say, we're going to destroy you!* But rather, we should approach each person as Christ would have—in love. If someone takes God's name in vain in our presence, rather than exploding at the person, say softly and sadly, "I wish you wouldn't use God's name in that way, for I love *Him*!" Tone can be everything.

The church members who were told they could not sing Christmas carols in the Parade of Lights made quite a statement the night of the parade. An hour and a half before the event kicked off, people starting gathering at a downtown plaza and then strolled down the city's streets, singing Christmas classics such as "Joy to the World," "The First Noel," and "Silent Night." By the time the caroling ended, shortly before the parade began, hundreds were singing at various street corners. The church also served gallons of hot chocolate to spectators. Many, non-Christians included, applauded the church's loving reaction to being banned from the parade.

What I am getting at is this: Every time we hear of another attempt to weaken the fiber of our nation, to eradicate all references to God or spiritual holidays such as Christmas or Easter, to put down families and individuals who are trying to live by the Mosaic yardstick, to sideline or ridicule the Bible, to change us by bombarding us with imagery and language that alienate us from God (however we conceptualize Him), what a difference we could make . . .

*If we'd just stand up!*

## THE FULLNESS OF TIME

I never cease to be amazed by God's incredible choreography. That God's timetable is so different from ours is never better illustrated than in the evolution of *Christmas in My Heart 14.*

It all started with my daily prayers: that God would determine what went between these two covers, not me. That God would write my Christmas story of the year, not me. That even the subject matter would be His. So it was that "By the Fireplace" was born. Second came the selection of the stories, always a wrenching process. From the first year the series began we have put together collections with broad thematic appeal. But now, for the first time in fourteen long years, I was impressed to do something we had never done before: choose only stories that fit within the framework of one theme: how family (both biological and of the spirit) handles tragedy or loss at Christmastime.

And so it was that, out of hundreds of top story candidates, God impressed me to choose only certain stories, a number that had been bridesmaids but never brides year after year, some for ten, eleven, twelve, even thirteen years! And now they fell into my lap like ripe apples. So why was it that year after year after year, I resignedly muttered, "Can't believe I'm rejecting this wonderful story again! How could I?" And finally this year, "Why does it fit now when it apparently didn't fit before?" Now I know.

## ABOUT THIS COLLECTION

Three of the authors represented are beloved of old by our readers. But it is always exciting to stir in writers whose voices we haven't heard before. And what a range of time periods are represented: Lanita Kampton (last quarter of the twentieth century), Harold Ivan Smith, Marjorie Yourd Hill, Dorothy Boys Kilian, and Katherine Reeves (mid-twentieth century), Earl Reed Silvers (first half of the twentieth century), and Hezekiah Butterworth (second half of the nineteenth century).

This is Pearl Buck's fifth appearance: her stories also appeared in our second, fourth, sixth, and tenth collections. It is Arthur Gordon's fourth appearance; his stories also appeared in our sixth, seventh, and eighth collections. It is also the fourth for Nancy Rue; her stories appeared in the seventh, ninth, and twelfth collections.

## CODA

I look forward to hearing from you! Please do keep the stories, responses, and suggestions coming—and not just for Christmas stories. I am putting together collections centered on other genres as well. You may reach me by writing to:

Joe L. Wheeler, Ph.D.
c/o Tyndale House Publishers
351 Executive Drive
Carol Stream, IL 60188

May the Lord bless and guide the ministry of these stories in your home.

# THE CHRISTMAS WISH

*The Bishop didn't think it was funny at all—in fact it bordered on the sacrilegious!*

*So the pastor apprehensively took the wishbone with him when he knocked on the door of the Jennisons' house. Perhaps someone there would tell him why a chicken wishbone was dropped in an offering plate.*

"I don't think it's funny," the Bishop said sharply. He stood up, and to the young Reverend Thomas Barlow he had never looked more imposing. "It's in bad taste. It's irreverent. It's—it's almost sacrilegious!"

Tom Barlow thought wretchedly that it did look odd: the great silver collection dish, the pile of bills and Christmas offering-envelopes, and in the middle, naked and unashamed, the wishbone of a large chicken.

"According to the usher," the Bishop said grimly, "this—this thing came from the Jennisons' pew. Well, the Jennisons may be as irreverent in their own home as they like, but this is the house of God!"

He moved over to the window where eddying snowflakes sifted gently. A white Christmas. Until now, a joyous Christmas. *Oh, why,* Tom Barlow asked himself, *did the Bishop have to preach his Christmas sermon here?*

The Bishop wheeled around. "Barlow, if these people talk about this indignity, the prestige of the church will suffer. I think you ought to see them personally and get an apology. This afternoon."

"*This afternoon,*" said the Bishop. "And take that object with you!"

The gleaming streets were decorated in honor of Christ's birthday, but driving through them, Tom Barlow felt no answering lift in his spirits. It was true enough that during his brief pastorate at Trinity Church he had been trying to attract people like the Jennisons: young, suave—the "cocktail set" some called them. It was also true that Cele Jennison looked like a fashion model, and Kirby Jennison had that careless assurance that sometimes made Tom Barlow feel uncomfortable. But sitting in church with their seven-year-old daughter, Lisa, beside them, they made a handsome sight.

One thing was certain: no apology would be forthcoming from the Jennisons. At best, they would laugh. At worst, they would be angry—and that would end their relationship with Trinity Church.

"Lord," whispered Tom Barlow in one of his sudden, unpremeditated prayers, "You'll have to help me with this. I don't have the slightest idea of how to handle it."

❄ ❄ ❄

The Christmas wreath on the door of the Jennisons' house was enormous; the festive tree in the living room glowed brightly. And yet, it seemed to Tom Barlow, there was an undercurrent of something: tension, friction, unhappiness. . . .

"A wishbone in the collection plate?" Cele Jennison burst out laughing. "Oh, how wonderful! I wish I could take the credit, but I can't. As for Kirby—that doesn't sound like him at all!"

Kirby Jennison shook his head. "Not guilty. You don't suppose Lisa . . ."

"Lisa?" Cele Jennison looked startled. "Well, we could ask her."

The child came in, sat down on the long sofa, hands tightly folded. When her mother put the question, she nodded mutely.

"But why?" said Kirby Jennison. "Why did you do it, Lisa?"

The child said softly, "I wanted God to help me with my Christmas wish."

"What wish?" Tom Barlow said.

The small voice was almost inaudible. "That Daddy and Mummy wouldn't fight. That we'd all be happy, the way we used to be."

Cele Jennison's eyes filled with tears. Kirby Jennison sat very still. It was the Reverend Mr. Barlow who finally moved.

He went to the child, who looked miserable and lost. From his pocket he took the wishbone. "To get your wish, Lisa, you have to pull it with somebody."

He beckoned to Cele Jennison. She came forward quickly. The snap of the wishbone was loud in the stillness.

"There," said Tom Barlow. "You've got the long end, Lisa. The long end gets the wish. And just to make *sure* . . ." He held his hand out to Cele Jennison. "Could I have your wedding ring, please?"

She stripped it off with fingers that shook a little. He took it and handed it to her husband. "Now, if you two will just stand together in front of the Christmas tree. . . ."

They obeyed him without question.

"Dearly Beloved, we are gathered together here in the sight of God, and in the face of this company . . ."

*Heavens*, a faint inner voice was saying to Tom Barlow, *the Bishop won't be getting his apology after all.* But he found, now, that it didn't matter. These were his people. By remarrying them in the sight of their child, he was helping them to the happiest Christmas of their lives.

## *Arthur Gordon*

(1912–2002)

During his long and memorable career, Arthur Gordon edited such magazines as *Cosmopolitan, Good Housekeeping*, and *Guideposts*. He was author of a number of books, including *Reprisal* (1950), *Norman Vincent Peale: Minister to Millions* (1958), *A Touch of Wonder* (1983), and *Return to Wonder* (1996), as well as several hundred short stories.

# A TREE FOR BENJI

---

*Why was his father so bullheaded in his refusal to permit a Christmas tree in his house? It just didn't make sense. And now, to break little Benji's heart!*

*He decided to have it out with his father once and for all.*

John Stevens rubbed his eyes as he stretched on the old couch in the living room. Today was December 21. Christmas was only four days away. Time was running out. How many times had eight-year-old Benji, his son, impatiently demanded, "When are we going to put up the tree?"

How could he tell him there wasn't going to be a tree this year? Last year—and the years before that—there had been a marriage, a reason to celebrate. Now . . . nothing. But that wasn't the real reason. There was that strange attitude of his dad, Benji's grandfather.

Eight months ago John had given up and moved in with his parents. Somehow, trying to pay the bills, care for the three boys, be father and mother, and deal with the gnawing hurt from the divorce demanded too much energy.

The old farmhouse, however, was overcrowded. His boys shared the tiny bedroom he had once shared with three brothers, and John longed for a bedroom now more than he had as a child.

Well, at least they were together. His mind went to Benji—the youngest child, the only one who kept talking about Jesus, and how He could do the impossible. Must have gotten that from some Sunday school. It certainly didn't run in the family. And how was Benji really dealing with the divorce? How many times had he asked about that tree?

John heard his father's telltale footsteps in the kitchen. The morning routine had not changed in decades. By the time John rolled out from under the covers, the coffee would be ready. Perhaps this was the morning to confront the old man about the tree.

He swung off the couch and shuffled into the kitchen.

"Morning," he said. His dad turned from the stove as though surprised to see him.

"Morning! Want some coffee?"

"Yeah, I better." John stretched again as he sat down to the same scarred table at which he had eaten almost every meal in his childhood. His dad placed a cup of steaming coffee in front of him, then slid the sugar and cream across the table.

"What's up today?" John asked.

"Thought I'd mend that fence." John noticed that his father assumed he knew which section. John pressed on.

"Soon be Christmas." The old man did not respond. John quickly took another sip of his coffee, seeking courage.

"Benji keeps asking when we're going to put up that tree. I don't know what to tell him."

A long silence followed. The old man drained the last of his coffee and stared at the bottom of his mug.

"Dad?" John pleaded.

"Ever been a tree that you can remember?" the old man said, jerking his gaze from the mug to his son.

"No, Dad. And that's just it. . . ." Abruptly, the elder Stevens stood and moved without effort to the sink. He placed the mug on the drain board and left the room.

John could not remember a Christmas tree in this house. For that reason, on the first Christmas of his marriage, he had squeezed the biggest tree he could find into their tiny apartment, mostly to spite the old man. His father had not even commented on it.

Why was his dad so against a Christmas tree? John

knew some people had religious objections, but his dad wasn't fond of churches.

He had not heard his mother's footsteps.

"Morning, Son," she mumbled. "Radio says it's fourteen degrees outside. When you leave for work, be sure and bundle up." She reached for her coffee mug and poured the coffee. Then she joined her son at the table. "How did you sleep?"

"Fine." That reply stretched the truth, but John didn't want to add another worry to his mom's overload.

"I'm concerned about your back, Son. . . ." John cut into the conversation, recycled from other mornings.

"Well, I've got more things than my back to worry 'bout." John stepped to the stove to pour another cup.

"Like Benji?" his mom asked.

"What about Benji? Has he been giving you problems?"

"That little guy's never a problem. But he sure is wanting a tree. That's all he talked about yesterday after he got home from school. A tree!"

"Well, I don't want him pestering you. . . ."

His mother cut him off. "Grandmothers delight in being pestered. He tells me most things on his mind. Eight-year-olds can't store much in their silos." She gestured toward her head. John moved his chair closer to his mother's.

"Mom, why hasn't there been a Christmas tree in this house?"

Before she spoke, his mother stroked a rough place on the tabletop. Then she said, "You asked me Benji's question every Christmas until you were ten." Her voice conveyed no trace of annoyance. "Funny . . .

Benji is so much like you . . . takes me back. He's the spitting image of you." John could not be certain if his mother was stalling or merely avoiding the question.

"Mom, why isn't there *a tree*?" John tried to keep the desperation from his voice.

"Same answer now as then. Just, 'cause."

"That's no answer for Benji. He's smart."

John's mother looked away, her eyes brimming. "Then I don't know! I never remember a tree, and I've lived in this house for forty years. Your dad don't like questions when he makes up his mind on something!"

"Did you ever ask him?"

"Once."

"What did he say?"

"Nothing. He just sat there in that rocking chair of his and stared at the wall."

John would have pressed the subject but chimes from the old clock on the fireplace mantle drifted into the kitchen, reminding him he was late. The questions would have to wait.

❄ ❄ ❄

Ten hours later, John pulled off the paved road and onto the gravel road that led to the farmhouse. He was exhausted from another day at the plant. Abruptly, Benji and his old mangy dog darted into his path. John stopped the car and rolled down the window.

"Been waiting for you," Benji said. "Wanna show you something." John took his foot off the brake and the car started moving. "No, Dad. I want to show you something!" Benji pleaded.

"What?" John snapped.

"Come on." Benji turned and bolted toward the woods. His dog barked once and followed. John turned the motor off and climbed out of the car. A blast of cold wind stung him. Whatever Benji wanted him to see must be important to risk this wind. Fortunately, Benji didn't run far.

"There it is." John couldn't follow his gesture.

"What, Benji?" he demanded impatiently.

"That's the one . . . that's the tree I want Granddad to put up for Christmas." The impact of the words were as raw as the December wind. "It's just right!" Benji proudly stated. John looked at a tree that would cost about twenty-five dollars in the city.

"Well, we'll have to think about it." The sentence escaped John before he considered its impact. He angrily kicked a frozen clod of dirt. Why not tell Benji the truth? There wasn't going to be a tree. He turned and walked rapidly toward the car.

"Dad?" Benji protested.

"Come on. Let's go. Grandma's got supper waiting." The little fellow turned for one last look at the tree.

They drove to the house in silence. If only Benji knew how many trees John had picked out before he quit trying to change his dad's mind.

John looked at his son huddled against the passenger door.

"What's wrong, pardner?"

"Nothing." But John recognized the hurt. Benji opened the door and ran toward the house.

John slammed his hand against the steering wheel,

more from frustration than anger. Now, he'd have to confront his dad in a way no son should.

❄ ❄ ❄

The house was again silent; the boys asleep. The three adults had silently watched TV. As the theme song of the late news announced the hour, John's father stood and remarked, "Getting late," his equivalent of "Good night."

"Dad, I need to talk to you. . . ." The old man switched off the TV. "Dad, Benji is wanting a Christmas tree. He's been through so much. And, well, I know this is your house and we're guests here, but how do I tell an eight-year-old, 'no tree'?"

There was a long silence. John couldn't be sure his mother was still in the room.

"Tell him there's never been a tree," the old man retorted too sharply for John's comfort. But still John thought he sensed a softening. He pressed on.

"He'll want to know why."

Another silence—this one longer. Then his father spoke slowly. "I was Benji's age. We'd gone down to the Perkins' place and cut the tree I'd picked out. It was a beauty. Back then we owned all that land. Pulled that tree home and put it up right there in that corner." He pointed toward the stairwell.

"We didn't have ornaments like most folk. Just popcorn strings and some ribbons. But it was pretty enough. My momma helped us string that popcorn and told us Christmas stories." The old man stopped. Only the ticking of the mantle clock broke the silence.

"Momma," the old man stopped again and cleared his throat. "Momma died that next day. Hadn't even been sick. She was the one who had trusted Jesus, and she was the one who died. I couldn't understand it all."

John edged forward on the couch because his father's words were whispered. "We didn't have funeral homes around here then. People were laid out at home. So, we had to take down the tree to put her casket there."

Suddenly, John's heart intertwined with his dad's. *How could an eight-year-old deal with that ugly invasion?* He saw his mother's tear-filled eyes dart from him to her husband.

"My momma was buried on Christmas Day . . . and I've never felt like celebrating."

After a moment John spoke, carefully struggling for words. "Dad, why didn't you tell me before now?"

"Every Christmas comes, I think about it. Can't seem to get it out of my mind," he said in his usual evasive way. Then the clock struck the half hour. As if on signal, the old man looked at the clock, then resumed his stoic posture. "Getting late," he said as he shuffled out of the room.

If John expected a comment from his mother, he was disappointed. "Turn out the lights, John, when you go to bed." But her words were spoken softly.

❄ ❄ ❄

Later, in the darkened room, John sat listening to the systematic tick-tick of the mantle clock. He turned to confront it. The clock had been a gift for his grandparents on their wedding day. How many other memories of that woman remained in this farmhouse to tease the eight-year-old child who cowered within the toughness of the sixty-nine-year-old farmer-father?

Finally, he punched the pillows in his nightly ritual. Tomorrow was December 22. Somehow he'd have to find a way to explain this to Benji. Although he didn't know much about the Bible, perhaps he could tie it into the Christmas story. Wasn't there something about a tree symbolizing eternal life? And Benji's great-grandmother had evidently been a believer. John turned restlessly, trying to fit the pieces together.

A few feet away, behind the security of the white bedroom door, tears trickled down the old man's face and wet the pillowcase. Sally Stevens had slept with this man for fifty years and had never seen a mood like this one. She called his name, but there was no response.

❄ ❄ ❄

The next afternoon, as Benji raced down the front steps of Martin Elementary School, he was greeted by a different horn. He discovered his granddad's old, exhausted '53 truck.

"Hi, Granddad," he said as he got in and pulled the rickety old door shut. The old man started the tired engine and pulled away from the curb.

"Have a good day, Boy?" the old man asked. Benji recited what a great time they had had this last day of school before the Christmas break. The truck sputtered along old bumpy roads heading home. When they turned down the lane leading to the woods, no explanation was offered or requested.

"See all that land over there, Boy?" the old man asked. "My daddy, your great-granddaddy, used to own all this. When I was your age I'd come down here and fight Indians." His voice gave the threat of danger.

"*Real* Indians?" Benji asked, his eyes the size of half-dollars. The old man laughed.

"No, Boy. Pretend Indians. This was my favorite place in the whole world." He pulled off the road and hopped out of the truck.

"Boy, you see that tree?" he raised his arm to identify a tall tree in a slump. Benji whispered, "Yes, sir."

"When I was your age I wanted to chop down that tree and take it home."

"But, Granddad, wasn't it awfully big to take home?"

"Ah, Boy," he said with a laugh. "It wasn't that big *then* . . . it was like, well, that one over there." Benji's eyes followed the old man's gesture to the very tree he had picked out the other day.

"Granddad," he exclaimed, "that would sure make a pretty Christmas tree!" After a moment he added, "Wouldn't it?"

From deep within the old man's spirit, the voice that responded was not that one tarnished by years of denial, but an eight-year-old boy's.

"Sure would, Boy. Sure would! Go get the ax . . . in the truck."

The old man swung the ax with the skill of years. One more solid swing of the ax would topple the cedar tree. The old man stopped. "Put out your hands, Boy."

Benji complied. "Here, you bring her down." Benji started to question. "You can do it—*your own Christmas tree.*"

Benji's eyes widened. His mind spun. *Imagine, cutting his own Christmas tree . . . no one else in his school could do that!*

Benji swung the ax. The tree swayed and fell slowly to the ground. Benji squealed with glee.

"Good job, Boy. Good job!"

❄ ❄ ❄

John knew what he would say—or at least what he *thought* he would tell Benji. For ten miles he had carefully rehearsed his lines. Hopefully, he had anticipated every question Benji would ask.

He got out of his car and walked toward the porch. Taking a deep breath, he opened the screen door and turned the old porcelain knob. His first thoughts were that he was in the wrong house. There stood a huge cedar tree filling the corner where he imagined another tree had once stood.

John looked to the old man for a word of explanation.

"Boy picked out a good one, didn't he?"

In that moment, father and son spoke a new language. Benji stared at them only a moment. Then he returned to hanging the ornaments his grandmother handed him.

"It's a tree for Benji," the old man said brightly, although his chin wobbled. "For Benji."

Then the final tears of a long season fell from the eyes

of a sixty-nine-year-old man who, as a boy, had also been called Benji.

*Harold Ivan Smith*

Harold Ivan Smith wrote for inspirational magazines in the mid-twentieth century.

Marjorie Yourd Hill

# SEA ANCHOR

---

*Coco was tired of living the humdrum life. Just the thought of being stuck on a dull island for Christmas when she could be enjoying high society with Fizz . . .*

*But Father and Mother— she just couldn't figure them out.*

If Father came at all, Coco was afraid, it would only be from a sense of duty. And that was hardly the spirit to start a winter holiday. You ought to feel enthusiastic, as the kids did. Coco watched the giggling capers of Janie and Tom—her sister, eleven, and brother, nine—and wished she could share their high spirits.

They were prancing around the wharf in constant danger of slipping into the icy sea, so excited about this winter visit to the island summer home (which they had not seen since before the war) that they had gone insane. The fact that Christmas was only four days away made them even crazier.

Mother had given up trying to calm them. She was sitting quietly inside the boat company's heated office, a gloved finger *tap-tap-tapping* on the arm of her chair and her lovely gray eyes seeking the island road again and again. The boat was due to leave for Spruce Island in half an hour, and Father was not here yet.

The three-man crew was loading mail and supplies for Spruce Village, with the help of Coco's fifteen-year-old brother, Peter. The northeast wind lashed the bay into steely waves. It was wild weather to be going out to the island. Greg, a year older than Coco and a freshman at Harvard, pulled his coat collar up as he paced the wharf uneasily.

He stopped beside Coco now and said, "Looks as if quite a storm is blowing up. We might have such a bad spell that the boat would stop running, and I couldn't get back for the New Year's Eve party with Doug and the gang."

"I know." Coco nodded, thinking of her own secret

plan. "I don't see why we couldn't have had this family reunion at some more accessible place."

She shivered and turned back into the grateful warmth of the office. Her mother flashed a nervous smile, and Coco felt a twinge of pity. Mother was always waiting. Maybe Father was never sure about the time and place because he was an artist. Maybe that's why their whole family life was odd.

Coco remembered family discussions last spring. They had been living at Grandmother Lawson's then, all except Greg and Peter, who were in prep school. In anticipation of Father's return to civilian life from the Army, Mother had achieved the miraculous: the promise of an apartment in New York City. Father, of course, would get back his old position with the McDuffy and Neal advertising agency.

Mother had not understood at first what Father meant when he said, "No," not "Of course."

"All right," she agreed reasonably, "there's Carmichael and Stratford. They're a bigger firm, anyway. Uncle Ned has connections there. He can get you in."

Father shook his head, his eyes tired. "That's just as bad. I mean I'd like to be through with all that for good."

"You mean give up your artwork completely?" Mother cried, and everybody at the table stared.

Father explained, "No, but I'd like to retrieve what I gave up years ago. I'm not sure that I can do it, but I want to take time out to give it a try."

Coco remembered vaguely that long ago Father had had a studio as a struggling young artist, but with five children to feed, clothe, and educate, he had been persuaded to accept the financial security of a job as art director of McDuffy and Neal. Now, it seemed, he regretted having given up his portrait painting and wanted to return to it again.

So the family plans were rearranged. Father set out alone for Taos to paint; Greg and Peter got jobs on a farm for the summer; Mother found an opportunity to act as housemother and counselor at a school which ran a summer camp, just the thing for her and the younger two. And Coco was disposed of simply by staying on at Grandmother's. Everybody seemed to like the arrangements except Coco, who considered herself stuck in a deadly hole and her life at a standstill.

Until she met Fizz Bates, that is. Fizz was in Mericassett visiting his married sister in his old hometown. Grandmother shook her head when Coco first mentioned him, so after that Coco discreetly said little about the rides in his roadster and the drugstore meetings. She kept his wonderful letters secret, too, and her latest scheme for the New Year holiday. She'd bring that up at a propitious moment. If Greg had freedom to go and come as he pleased, she could, too. If everyone in the family was going his own way and leading his own life, she would, too. This idea of a family reunion in midwinter, on an island inhabited only by a score or so of fishing families, was preposterous.

Mother had insisted on it, though. Not Grandmother's horrified exhortations nor the wagging of Mericassett tongues had stopped her. Only Father's refusal to come could have caused the plan to fall through. Mother had explained herself at Grandmother's only yesterday when she brought Janie and Tom down from boarding school.

Coco was stacking the luncheon dishes in the kitchen, but when she caught a queer note in Mother's voice she stopped scraping and piling.

Mother said with a little catch in her breath, "But, Mother, you don't understand! This family just has to be together again in our own home before it's too late. We've lived around so much with other people during the war and after, and been so separated, that I think—well, if we don't get together in a place of our own soon—" The rest of the sentence sounded as if stopped by a sob.

Coco silently slid a Haviland cup off its saucer and meticulously dumped out a few tea leaves. Her own throat felt tight, but she told herself it was already too late. Weren't they all set on lives of their own choosing—both she and Greg, as well as Father?

But she couldn't help wondering now if it had been fear of just that which had made Mother so worried.

The captain barged in, scowling at a sheaf of papers.

"You the lady ordered the Franklin stove from Searles for your house out on the island?"

Mother nodded.

"It ain't here. Checked over everything settin' on the pier."

Coco's eyes widened at this complication. They needed the stove to supplement the fireplace and kitchen range. Otherwise the house would be uninhabitable.

"Oh, dear!" Mother murmured helplessly. "What shall I do?"

"Whyn't you just cancel the order? It's too late now to do you any good. Bert Mahoney said, when it weren't on the load Monday, he'd haul up his grandma's old stove—been settin' in his shed nineteen years—and warm your place up with it. He's had fires goin' two days now, and the house is snug. That old place o' Captain Wilcox' always did heat well."

Mother relaxed, and Coco took a deep breath. So the friendly Spruce Villagers were looking after them, as they had in former summers!

Suddenly the children began to scream. "He's here! He's come! Hi, Daddy, hi! Here we are!"

Father scrambled out of a taxi and braced himself for the onslaught of Janie and Tom, who hung on him so that he had to kiss Mother over their heads. He stretched out a hand to Coco and the older boys.

"Hi, everybody," he grinned. "My train was held up by snowstorms farther west, but here we are, all together at last."

The captain touched his visor. "It's a good thing you're makin' this sailin', because from the look of things we mayn't be makin' another trip for a while—maybe a week or ten days."

Coco and Greg exchanged uneasy looks. That would ruin their plans.

One thing stood out in Coco's mind in all the kaleidoscopic events of that homecoming day, and that was the moment she stood with her parents on the porch while Father fumbled with the keys. Janie and Tom were racing around the yard, exploring, while Greg and Peter lugged suitcases up the winding stone walk that led from the road.

"Seven years," Father said half under his breath, "I've carried this key all over the earth, and there were times I thought I'd never use it again. But thank goodness, Viv, I'm back here again at last. Are you glad, too?"

Coco had to turn away from the shining soft look on Mother's face. But she couldn't help hearing, though she pretended to be absorbed solely in Peter's struggle with three suitcases.

"Of course. It's going to be the answer to everything, Russ."

"It's your spirit that keeps me going, Viv, standing out against your critical family and the whole doubting world. It's all I've got to count on, really."

"Except yourself," Mother said firmly. "Here in this lovely spot, where we've all had such fun together, I know things will work out, Russ."

Arm in arm, Mother and Father stepped inside. Peter hurled the three suitcases on the porch and went back for the last. Janie and Tom pounced on them, squealing, and dragged them through the door. Coco stood alone on the porch, blinking a mist from her eyes.

It was silly, it was sentimental nonsense, that an old place where you had once spent your summers could do this to you. The house wasn't even very attractive, especially in the bleak, winter late-afternoon light. It needed paint, and a shutter was missing, and the front steps sagged ominously. But there were lights in all the windows, and gay voices inside, and its warm cheer evoked pleasant memories of the happy past.

But the past had vanished, and it was ridiculous to recall the sunset walks hand in hand with Father along the shore, when just to be with him made you feel so secure. It was foolish to tingle at the remembrance of the heavenly smell of the wild raspberry patch in the hot sun, where you all picked and laughed and joked together; or the delicious clambakes on the beach that ended after starlight; or the swims; or the sailboating.

*I'm beyond all that,* she argued with herself. *I have nothing in common with the rest of the family now. I must make my own life.*

This idea became an obsession that kept her from entering into the holiday preparations. Their stay would be snug, thanks to Bert Mahoney's grandma's stove. Father and the boys cut holes in the ceiling to let heat upstairs to the two bedrooms, one for the girls, and one for their parents.

The three boys pulled mattresses up close to the stove to sleep.

The family made quite a ceremony about cutting their own Christmas tree and bringing in the Yule log. Mother had the oven always filled with spicy-smelling baking. On Christmas Day, Coco kept telling herself that she was too old for that sort of thing, but she couldn't help enjoying the homemade presents, sticky candy, and childish decorations of crayoned Santa Clauses. When it was over, she resolved, she would speak about her plans. However, the right moment never seemed to come.

It kept on snowing, and the island took on the look of a Christmas card. The kids went coasting. Even Greg shed his dignity and seemed to enjoy himself, but when the Mahoney boy knocked at the door and shyly asked Coco if she cared to try out his new toboggan with him, she smiled regrets and watched him plod away.

Let them all enjoy these childish pastimes—though how tall and good-looking that Bill Mahoney had grown since the last summer they had waded in tide pools, looking for starfish together! But let him go. Coco had other plans. When Greg took the boat to the mainland tomorrow, she was going, too. She had already put her best clothes in her suitcase.

Two weeks as a guest at Fizz's married sister's house, when he would be there for his college vacation—that was what she had planned. Surely her parents could not be unreasonable about that. Coco had had a letter from Sybil inviting her to stay there. Once away from home, she could begin to lead her own grown-up life, unhampered by family ideas that she was still a child. Fizz had written glowingly of the New Year's Eve ball at the country club, and other dances.

As Coco sat by the big picture window, dreaming of glamorous days and nights, her father wandered into the room and stopped abruptly when his eyes fell on her, as if struck by something.

"Stay right where you are, Coco," he said intensely, "'til I get my painting gear. That pose reminds me—"

What started as a quick sketch turned into a full painting. At last Father told Coco they'd better stop but he'd like to try it again tomorrow. "I'll call it *Portrait of a Girl Dreaming*."

Coco told herself that this was the time to speak up and tell him what was on her mind. Tomorrow she wouldn't be here. But she said nothing aloud, except falteringly, "You said the pose reminded you of something, Father. I've been wondering what."

He looked at her for a long time before he spoke, and

finally, with a softening light in his eyes, he said, "Your mother—the first time I painted her just after we were married. It was in Paris, and I was there on a fellowship, and we were terribly poor, but awfully happy, even though her family wasn't too keen about her marriage to a practically penniless artist.

"That picture was my first big success. It won a prize at an exhibition, and a South American millionaire bought it for what at that time was a fabulous sum."

He hesitated, then continued thoughtfully, "It had a quality I've never been able to catch again 'til now, seeing you. If I can get it down, Coco, I'll know I've not lost my ability. I'd like to make it larger, though, and the sea background more evocative."

"Won't that take a long time?" Coco's voice sounded extremely faint.

"Can't say," Father declared cheerfully. "Two or three weeks maybe." Then, her attitude penetrating his consciousness, he looked at her wonderingly. "You don't mind, Kitten, do you? I won't keep you sitting more than an hour or so a day."

Coco's tongue seemed to stick to the roof of her mouth. She said nothing, and her father picked up his things, thinking her silence meant consent. She slipped away with an anguished heart. Father needed her, it was true, but just as a model, nothing more. Would she have to sacrifice her cherished scheme for a painter's whim? She could hardly sit quietly at dinner and listen to Greg talk about his plans for the trip tomorrow.

"The captain says it's calming, and he hopes to put out by 9 a.m. Doug wants me to stay with him till classes begin, but I don't know. I may come back after the weekend and finish out the vacation with you."

Greg smiled engagingly, with a little-boy dimple in his cheek. "It's more fun than I expected here, and if I hadn't already promised the gang—"

Mother beamed at him. "We'd like you with us, Greg, you know that. But you're the oldest, and branching out now, so if you want to be with your college friends, we'll understand."

Coco suddenly choked on a cinnamon bun. With everyone's attention focused on her, she wondered wildly why she didn't simply stand up and declare that she, too, was old enough to branch out.

After Tom and Peter had thumped her on the back, she excused herself and went to her room.

Next morning she was too miserable to go down and say good-by to Greg, but she heard it all.

Father sounded grave. "I don't like the look of the sea."

"I know, but the captain knows his stuff, and if he sails, I'll go along," declared Greg.

Mr. Mahoney honked, and Greg was off. By and by Coco pulled herself together and went down. Later in the morning she took the usual pose for her father, who worked in silent absorption, squinting at his daughter as if she were a stranger.

What was growing on the canvas was strange to Coco. Her pictured self surprised her. *Portrait of a Girl Dreaming* was Coco as her father must see her, fresh and sweetly wistful. It was not the grown-up, sophisticated personality she had been trying to make of herself. *Could she,* Coco wondered gropingly, *have been mistaken about what sort of person she was?*

The other members of the family stopped to admire. Mother stood a long time before it, "It really has something, Russ. It will bring recognition again."

Father paused, brush in air. "It will be a canvas I can show the Institute Committee when they interview me next month for that teaching position."

Coco restrained a desire to bounce up and ask questions. If Father taught somewhere, they could all have a home together. It would mean security, without the sacrifice of Father's ambition.

"It took being here—all together in this old house—to put me in this mood again. I was beginning to be afraid that I'd lost it forever."

Coco's mother's face looked rosy and young, exactly like the portrait, as she laid her hands on her husband's shoulders. "We're all getting back something we feared we'd lost forever. Even the children. Isn't that so, Coco?" Her bright smile enfolded her daughter.

Coco could only smile back, a lump in her throat. *Grown-ups*, she thought, *talking like that!* Why, her parents were people struggling and learning, like herself. They weren't the fixed and solid demigods of her childhood, nor the disappointing idols with feet of clay of later years, but just people. Her father, who had been driven by circumstances out of his natural bent, was striving to get back again, without Coco's understanding or helping very much until now.

At the sound of stomping feet on the porch she looked out. There was Greg back, and Bill Mahoney.

"Captain's not sailing! Sea's still too heavy, though it's clearing. I may not even bother to make the trip tomorrow. It's a long way down to Boston just for a party. Think I'll spend New Year's Eve with the crowd here."

Bill stood just inside the door, looking red and eager, his eyes never leaving Coco's face. "We're planning a skating party at our pond, with cider to toast the New Year in around a bonfire. Will you come too, Coco?"

Coco looked at him, and at Greg, and a weight flew off her heart. She caught her breath. "I'd love it!"

Then, unexpectedly, she felt her lips tremble—with happiness, she supposed—and her eyes brimmed. It was silly of her, and she looked quickly out the window to hide her emotion.

The storm clouds were passing, rolling rapidly out to sea on a northwest wind. Half the sky was already blue, and sunlight shone upon the snow-covered island and the pounding sea. For a moment it was even more beautiful than in summer. It was like some of those quick flashes of insight you had sometimes when you thought about life.

You had to be where you could have vision, but you needed an anchor, too. Like this house—it was their sea anchor. It gave them both vision and security. Coco, her heart joyous, turned her eyes from the infinity of waves and sky in toward the warm firelit room that held her family and friend.

"Hold that expression, Coco!" shouted Father, searching wildly among his tubes for some more white to squeeze on his palette. "That's the look I want. Now if I can only convey the light—"

*Marjorie Yourd Hill*

Marjorie Yourd Hill wrote for popular magazines in the early to mid-twentieth century.

# THE SOFT SPOT IN B606

*The prisoner was feared for his violence. No one trusted him an inch. Then, one cold Christmas day, in walked a small, frail eleven-year-old girl.*

*This very old story from England has been patiently waiting in our story archives for fourteen long years. Its time has come.*

Bells were pealing faintly, somewhere in the distance, when B606 was released from the punishment cells. Somewhere there was merriment and chiming of bells—but not in the great grim walls of the English prison; not in the grim, hardened heart of convict B606.

B606, for the five days just past, had been on bread and water in one of the punishment cells. He had been violent, and abusive to one of the wardens. B606 was a "tough 'un." In Portland Prison no one was more closely watched in the sullen gray-coat ranks.

"Merry Christmas," someone chanted in his ears as he shuffled into line with his mate on the parade ground. A loud laugh followed, as if it were a good joke to be merry at Christmas in Portland Prison. But the man—he was still a man—with the round badge marked with B606 on his gray jacket, started discernibly at the sound of the two words in his ear. Under the hard mask of his sullen face something like pain worked dimly. When had he heard those two words before? Who had said them in his ear years ago?

"Front rank, two paces to left—march!" The governor of the prison strode about, giving low-voiced orders to the guards. His keen, shaven face was softened a little by the Christmas "peace, good will" that had crept into it. He laughed out cheerily now and then, and spoke a kind word to some numbered convicts in the lines. At the sight of B606 the stern lines tightened about his lips again. The Christmas look vanished. "Keep a look-out, Charlie," he muttered to the nearest warden. "He's a slippery one. There's blood in his eye today. No knowing how *he'll* celebrate Christmas."

"He's loony," growled the warden, surlily. "Twon't

no ways inconvenience me when he slings his hook. They ain't no soft spot in 'im."

"Well, keep a look-out awhile longer, Charlie. Watch out sharp. He'll be out in a matter of six months now."

What's six months' time to nine years and a half? But nevertheless, B606 felt no exultation. He had long since ceased to count off the months on his fingers. It did not matter one way or another that he was almost "out." The old despair and numbness in his heart had deadened hope long since.

The day lagged on inside the walls of Portland Prison. Outside it was merry Christmas, and the people made merry among their own.

In the afternoon the chief warden approached the convict in the blue cap with the number B606 on his jacket, with a message from the governor. He was wanted at the receiving office. B606 strode along beside the warden indifferently. It did not occur to him to wonder at the unusual summons. It could only mean some fresh punishment—it didn't matter.

They had arrived at the receiving office. A little child was standing there beside a calm-faced Sister of Charity. The convict stared at them both in dull wonder. But at the sound of the child's voice he started violently.

"Merry Christmas, Daddy!" The slender little figure crossed to him and slipped a small brown hand into his hand. "Won't you say 'Merry Christmas' back, Daddy? It was such a piece of work to get here. I guess you'd never think how hard it was to get an order to come! It was the Sister who did it. You see, she promised Mother to bring me. Mother's dead."

For a moment it was silent in the dismal room. The

governor turned away to gaze out the window, and the warden's rough face softened. The childish voice began again: "She tried to wait, Daddy—guess you'd never think how hard she tried! But when she knew she couldn't, she got everything ready for you and told me to wait instead. I'm waiting now, Daddy—it's lonesome—you'd never think how lonesome it is!

"But I keep counting the days off. Every night I cross one out. You can begin to expect when there's only a hundred an' eighty-six. When it's only one day left—my, think of that, Daddy! Mother used to. An' I know just what I'm going to do then—just exactly! Mother and I used to practice together. She told me just how I was to tidy up the kitchen, an' get the kettle all ready to boil, and be sure to remember the chair you always like to sit in—an' the g-ranium! Oh Daddy, Mother and I used to hope so it would be in bloom that day! She said for me to put on a new white apron, an' stretch up tall, and smile. I guess you'd never think how much we practiced. The last time Mother cried a little, but that was because she was so tired—I cried, too. It was that night Mother died. I—it's very lonesome now, Daddy, but I'm waiting. You'll come right home, won't you, Daddy?"

The great hard fingers had closed around the small brown ones. The tears were trailing over the rough cheeks of B606. The Sister's calm face was broken into lines of weeping.

"I'm most twelve now, Daddy. You mustn't mind how little I am—I can stretch up tall! An' you'll laugh to see how I can keep house for you. There's a woman on the third floor helps me when I forget how Mother said to do. I've got a hundred and eighty-six days more to practice in, Daddy. Daddy, won't you say 'Merry Christmas'?"

❄ ❄ ❄

The New Year came and grew on familiar terms with the world. Spring crept into the lanes and turned them green, and even the files of gray-coated convicts at their quarrying drew in the warm, sweet breaths and, in their way, rejoiced. The heart of one of them lightened within him as day followed day. On the walls of his cell he crossed off each one as it passed, and counted eagerly those that were left. They grew to be very few.

He practiced the home-going over and over, alone in his cell. It kept him happy and softened the fierce, angry light in his eyes. He grew peaceable and quiet among his mates. The wardens talked of it in amazement.

One summer day, B606 "went out." Across the strip of sea a child was waiting for him. The room was tidied and the kettle put on to boil, and in the sunny window the geranium was all in bloom. A new life had begun, and the prison shackles fell away from him. He was no longer B606. He was a man among men, and a child's love and faith strengthened him.

# THE NIGHT MY FATHER CAME HOME

*Few Christmas stories are told from a child's perspective; this is one of those rare ones.*

*Al was old—twenty-five or so—and crabby. Very crabby. Sad, too. All because of a letter.*

*But Joe persisted. He had a letter too.*

❄ ❄ ❄

*(This old story is so rare that, in all my searching through the years, I have only found two copies; from the synthesis of the two I have arrived at this edited text).*

My mother said he was gone for good, but I thought if I wrote to Santa Claus . . .

As soon as I wrote the letter I went down to the post office to mail it, so it would get there in time. Boy, there were about a million people standing in line and everything, and inside there was all that Christmas music coming out of a big horn on the wall.

Pretty soon I found the place in the wall where you put letters in, but it was too high up. So I went out again and I went around to the back of the post office, where there were these big doors open and a man was carrying boxes out to a truck. There must have been a million boxes. I never saw so many.

There was nobody there but him. He was kind of tall and thin and his face was dirty from where he kept rubbing his hand across it. He had freckles and his ears stuck out. I don't know how old he was. Pretty old. Twenty-five, I guess, like my father. He kept picking up these boxes and throwing them on the truck, and he didn't see me, so I yanked on his coat.

"Here's a letter," I said. "The place out there where you're supposed to put it in is too high up."

He was lifting this big box, and he stopped and looked at me. It was kind of a mad look. Then he looked down at the letter and he made a noise like my father the time he never saw this skate I left in the hall until he kind of slid downstairs on it.

"That's what I've been waiting for," he said. "A letter to Santa Claus." He kind of groaned. "It might interest you to know that we have sent out 143,000 pieces of mail in the past week and that there will be at least twice that much in the next three days before Christmas. This makes my day complete."

I was glad he was glad even if he didn't look so happy. He didn't take the letter, so I held it out again. "Will it get there right away?" I said. "It's important."

"How old are you?" he said. He still sounded mad.

"Six," I said. "Well, five."

"What's your name?" he said.

"Joe," I said.

"Look, Joe," he said. He sure looked like he was going to yell at me, but all of a sudden he didn't, like my father the time I took his shaving soap to make some frosting for my mud pies. "Joe, I can't take your letter," he said. "Believe me. It won't go any place. . . . I mean Santa Claus has already left the North Pole, see, so he can't get any more letters. So just take it back to your folks. They'll take care of it for you."

He didn't understand anything. "Look, I haven't got folks," I said. "I mean I've got a mother, but she works in a store all day and I have to stay with Mrs. Henderson next door all the time after I get back from school. That's what I wrote in the letter. I want my father to come home."

"Where'd he go?" He looked at me kind of funny, like he was waiting for something. He was sure dumb.

"He just went away," I said. "He just got hurt in an accident and then he went away. My mother said he won't ever come back anymore, but I want to surprise her. He's got to come back for Christmas, on account of he promised I would get some marbles and a baseball glove and a football and an electric train. Last year I wasn't old enough, but I am now."

The way he acted, you'd think he didn't hardly even listen to what I said. He didn't even say anything. He just kept on looking at me, and after awhile he kind of shrugged.

"Look, Joe," he said. He sounded real tired all of a sudden. "I'm busy. I'm sorry. Go home, will you? I can't take your letter."

"Sure you can," I said. "It's got a stamp on it." What was the matter with him anyway? He was starting to pick up all those boxes again, so I just put it on this table where there were about a million letters and I walked out.

"I'll be back pretty soon," I said. "Tomorrow—I guess there'll be an answer by tomorrow for sure."

I could hardly wait, thinking how surprised my mother was going to be and everything. So the next day, as soon as the school bus let me out at the corner at noon, I ran down to the post office. There were some other people moving boxes around in this big room, so I just kind of walked around the edge until I saw him in another little empty room. He was sitting on a box, eating his lunch.

"Did I get a letter yet?" I said. I was kind of out of breath. He let out a big groan when he saw me standing there, and he kept right on eating this big sandwich. His face was still dirty. He looked madder than ever.

Pretty soon he gave this big sigh, like my father did once when I cut up his pajamas for a Halloween costume. "As a matter of fact," he said, "a letter did turn up this morning addressed to somebody named 'Joe.' And nobody . . . nobody . . . could have been more surprised than I was."

"I knew it!" I said. "I told you so!" It was for me, all right. I could see my name "Joe" on the envelope, but there was a lot of writing, like typewriting, on the paper inside, so I gave it back to him. I was in a hurry.

"I can't read writing very well," I said. "You read it. Hurry up! I told you he was coming home."

"Now wait a minute, Joe," he said. "Let's wait and see what the letter says."

I could hardly wait. I kept kind of jumping up and down, I was in such a hurry. "Sit down, will you?" he said.

I sat down on this box beside him. He began to read kind of fast and running the words together:

*Dear Joe:*

*Thank you for your letter. I wish I could make sure that your father would be home for Christmas but I'm afraid I can't, so please don't count on it. However, I hope you have a Merry Christmas.*

*Very truly yours,*
*Santa Claus*

"Is that all?" I said. "There must be more. Maybe you dropped the other part somewhere. Look around, will you?"

He let out another big groan. "As a matter of fact," he said, "now that you mention it, I guess I did forget one thing. Some marbles turned up here this morning addressed to somebody named 'Joe.' I guess they're for you too."

He reached in his pocket and pulled out this sack of marbles. Boy, they were real good marbles and everything, and I was sure glad to get them. But I was still worried about the letter. "I guess I better hurry up and write another letter," I said. "You can mail it for me like you did before. I guess I didn't say how important it was. Anyway, I want to thank him for the marbles."

"That won't be necessary," he said. "I give you my personal guarantee that there is no point in writing another letter."

"This time you write it," I said. "You can make it sound better. Thank him for the marbles and tell him how important it is that my father comes home, and not to forget the rest of the things I'm supposed to get, like the baseball glove and the football and the electric train. Mail it right away, will you?"

"Joe," he said, "you're a determined man. So am I. Right now I am eating my lunch." He took out this big ham sandwich.

"Is that a ham sandwich?" I said.

"Yes," he said.

"Is it good?" I said.

"Yes," he said. He looked at me kind of mad and he kept on chewing real hard, and then he took another ham sandwich out of the bag. "Could I possibly persuade you to join me?" he said.

"Sure," I said. It was good, too. I was hungry.

"What's your name?" I said.

"Al," he said.

Pretty soon we finished the sandwiches. Then he took out this big red apple and started to eat it.

"My father used to cut up apples with his penknife," I said.

"I'll *bet* he did," Al said. "I'll bet he *had* to, in self-defense."

I watched Al cut up the apple, and we ate it for a while.

"How come you don't want to write this letter for me?" I said. "Don't you know how to write a letter?"

All of a sudden Al threw the apple core clear out the door to the alley.

"I know how to write a letter, all right," he said. "I just don't know how to get the right answers." Maybe there was a worm in the apple or something. He sure looked funny.

"How come?" I said. "You mean you don't think you're going to get what you want for Christmas either?"

"You might put it that way," Al said. "Only in the Army we called it a 'Dear John' letter."

Boy, did he look crabby all of a sudden, like this big lion, the time my father took me to the zoo, that had a toothache and tried to bite everybody.

"What's a 'Dear John' letter?" I said. "Is it good or bad?" I guess it was this letter that made him look so mad all the time, all right. Now he picked up an orange and threw it out the door, without even eating it or anything. What was the matter with him, anyway?

"Let's just skip it, Joe," he said pretty soon. "All it means is that a girl married somebody else."

"Girls are sure dumb," I said. "Playing with dolls and kissing people and everything. I hate girls."

"Hold that thought, Joe," Al said. "It may come in handy later on."

"If you're in the Army, how come you work in the post office?" I said.

"I got rotated home last month," Al said. "I needed a job. The post office needed an extra clerk for the Christmas rush. We were made for each other."

He crumpled up his lunch bag and threw it out the door. Boy, he sure had a good aim. I bet he could have been a big-league pitcher or something if he wanted to. "Look, Joe," he said. "Recess is over. If you have plans for this afternoon, don't let me detain you."

"Well, I guess I better get home, on account of Mrs. Henderson will have a fit," I said. "Don't forget to write the letter right away. Make it a good one. I'll be back tomorrow."

Al kind of groaned again, like my father the time my white rat made a nest in his bedroom slipper.

"Look, Joe," he said, "we've just been through all this. Take my word for it, it's a lost cause. I can't possibly write the letter."

"Sure you can," I said. "I'll pay you back for the stamp and everything out of this money I saved up for Christmas. Send it airmail."

I came right back after school the next day, and Al was eating his lunch again in this kind of empty room. He didn't even look up when I came in. He was eating a fried-egg sandwich.

"Where's the letter?" I said. "Does it say my father is coming for sure?"

Al just kept on eating. He had kind of a fried-egg mustache.

"Didn't it come yet?" I said. "There's only one more day until Christmas."

"Look, Joe," Al said. "Let's not kid ourselves. I told you there wouldn't be any letter."

"Maybe it just didn't get here yet," I said. "Wasn't there even a bag or a box or anything, like last time when he sent the marbles?"

Al let out this big long sigh. "As a matter of fact," he said, "now that you mention it, I do remember finding this paper bag with your name on it. There seems to be some kind of big glove in it." He gave me this old wrinkled paper bag.

"That's the baseball glove!" I said. "Don't you even know that?" Boy, was he dumb. It was about a million times too big, but it was sure a good glove. "That's one of the things I'm supposed to get for Christmas," I said. "Don't you remember? I already told you. There were the marbles and the baseball glove and a football and an electric train. . . ."

"I know," Al said. "Just don't keep reminding me."

"Is that a fried-egg sandwich?" I said.

Al gave it to me and took out another one.

"Joe, I'm eating my lunch," he said. "I mean, we're eating my lunch. Don't you ever get anything to eat at school?"

"You're not supposed to eat anything at school!" I said. He sure didn't know anything. "You're supposed to learn things. Didn't you ever go to school?"

"Off and on," Al said. "What things are you supposed to learn?"

"Drawing and things," I said. "I'm in kindergarten. What were you supposed to learn?"

"Drawing and things," Al said. "I was going to be an architect."

"I bet that would be fun," I said. "What is it?"

"It's somebody who builds things," Al said. "Like houses and so forth." He took out this big banana and peeled it, and I helped him eat it.

"I sure wish we had a house," I said. "Can you build one?"

"First you have to learn how," Al said.

"Then why don't you learn how?" I said.

All of a sudden Al threw the banana peel clear out the door to the alley. He was beginning to look mad again. "Look, Joe," he said. "It's a long grind. That was a long time ago. I had a lot of plans then that never worked out." All of a sudden he took out this big candy bar and ate the whole thing before I could even say anything. "I've got a whole new set of problems now," he said. "Like finding another job after Christmas."

"What kind of job?" I said.

"Any kind of job," Al said. "Who cares? What difference does it make?"

"You're sure you don't want to build a house?" I said. "So you could have a dog in the backyard and everything? I sure like dogs."

All of a sudden Al threw the whole lunch bag out the door, without even eating the rest of it or anything. "Look, Joe," he said. "I don't want to build a house. I don't want to be an architect. I don't want to have a dog in the backyard."

Boy, he sure did look crabby now, like that big lion at the zoo that kept roaring and jumping up and biting people when that man tried to fix his toothache.

"Listen, Joe," he said. "I've got to get back to work. You've got to go home. Let's just skip the whole thing. Go play with your marbles."

So then he went back in this big room with all the boxes, and he went inside one of these cages where people sell stamps and everything. He shut the door, but I could tell which cage it was on account of it said STAMPS on the glass bar. There wasn't hardly anybody in this big room, so I went around the edge until I got to his door and I opened it real quiet. There were about a million people lined up on the other side of the cage, waiting to buy some stamps and everything.

"Hey, Al," I said. "We forgot to look for the letter. I'll come back tomorrow and help you find it."

Al turned around and looked at me. He looked madder than ever. I mean real mad, like my father the time I dropped his watch in the bathtub. "Let's face it, Joe," he said. "There isn't going to be any letter. I'm sorry, but sometimes you just don't get what you want for Christmas."

"You do if you want it hard enough," I said. "My father said so. He said we would have a real big Christmas tree this year, and underneath there would be the marbles and the baseball glove and the football and the . . ."

"Listen, Joe," Al said. "I've done all I can. I'm sorry, believe me. Run along now, will you? Get lost. I just haven't got any more time to play games."

Who asked him to play games, anyway? All of a sudden the door to the cage shut with a bang right in front of me. I guess it blew shut or something. So I went home.

The next day it was Christmas Eve, only not until that night, you know what I mean. I didn't get to go to the post office after school, on account of Mrs. Henderson picked me up, but pretty soon I sneaked out while she was baking some cookies and she thought I was taking a nap.

I guess it was pretty late, all right; it was almost dark by the time I got there. It was sure cold. The back door to the post office was locked. I couldn't even open it. So I came around the side and there was somebody sitting on the steps. It was Al. He still looked mad, like my father the time I got lost at the circus. He was sort of shivering and his face looked kind of blue. "What are you doing here?" he said. "You're late."

"I was looking for you," I said. "My mother said last night that my father really isn't going to come home for Christmas, no matter what. She said I shouldn't of bothered you. I'm sorry I bothered you."

"Think nothing of it," Al said. "Everything bothers me." He gave me this kind of lumpy-looking big bag. "I just thought I'd better make sure you got this package that came for you today. It looks like it's got some kind of a ball in it."

"That's a football!" I said. Boy, it was a real football, like they use in a football game and everything. "Thanks for waiting," I said. I sat down beside him on the steps. It was pretty cold, all right. . . .

"Joe," Al said, "why don't you go home?" He looked like my father the time I put this real swell lizard I found once on his plate at dinner. "Doesn't anybody pay any attention to where you are?"

"Sure they pay attention," I said. "They think I'm

asleep. My mother has to work late tonight until nine o'clock in the store, and she said afterwards she's going to go out again and get the Christmas tree. Only the thing is, I'm going to surprise her. I'm going to get this big tree and put it up like my father always does, so we can put the electric train under it."

"*What* electric train?" Al said.

"The one I wrote about in the letter. Only it hasn't got here yet."

"I wouldn't count on it," Al said. "You can't be too sure about getting things. For example, you need an electric train, but I need a new suit. One of us is apt to be disappointed."

"It'll come, all right," I said. "Everything else did. It'll probably be there when I get back home. Do you like to pick out Christmas trees and put the ornaments on and everything?"

"No," Al said.

"I never bought a Christmas tree before," I said. "I went with my father. But I guess it's easy, all right."

"Have you got any money?"

"Sure I've got money," I said. I guess he thought I was dumb or something. "I had almost a dollar saved up, and I spent fifty cents for a present for mother, so I've got thirty-five cents left."

All of a sudden Al looked like he was getting mad again, or tired or something. "Look, Joe, just go home, will you?" he said. "Forget about the Christmas tree and the electric train. Get a good night's sleep."

"I will," I said. "First I want to get the tree, so I can put the electric train under it."

I started down this street where I saw this big place

where they sell Christmas trees, but I couldn't hardly even see the post office, it was too dark. So I kept on going.

Pretty soon I heard somebody in back of me. It was Al. "Hey, Joe!" he said. He had this kind of funny look on his face, like my father the time I made this big Father's Day card for him at school and brought it home. "I just happened to think of a fellow I know who sells Christmas trees," Al said. "I saw some big ones there for about thirty-five cents.

"Well, it was down this way," Al said. "But if you don't mind waiting, I've got an errand to do first in the hardware store."

Al told me to wait outside the hardware store, and he was in there for a pretty long time, but I didn't mind waiting on account of there was this electric train set up in the window with tracks and bridges and tunnels and everything. It sure was a swell train.

It was a good thing Al came along when I bought this Christmas tree at this place he knew for thirty-five cents, on account of I couldn't even carry the tree, it was so big. Al had to carry it. I helped him some. It sure smelled good.

It was a pretty long walk home. By the time we got there this truck was stopped out in front and a man was just putting a big box in front of our door in the hall.

"That's my electric train," I said. "I told you it would get here."

"That's right," Al said. "Now that I think of it, you did tell me."

Mrs. Henderson was sure mad when she saw I had sneaked out and everything, but Al said he would get me some supper, so after a while she unlocked the door to our apartment and we went inside. Boy, the tree I bought was too big, even, but it fitted fine after Al cut off the top of the tree like my father used to do.

It turned out this electric train was so big it ran all around the living room. First we put down the tracks and the bridges and the tunnels and the trestle and the freight cars and the engine and the passenger train and the caboose. Then Al put all these ornaments we had on the tree while I put the marbles and the baseball glove and the football underneath, like they were supposed to be.

He just put this big star on the top of the tree when my mother came in. Boy, was she surprised. She looked kind of tired and messed up and she was carrying all these packages.

"This is Al," I said.

My mother looked at Al and he looked at her, and all of a sudden they kind of smiled. Her face got all red and she sort of just stood there.

"Well, this certainly is kind of you," my mother said. Her voice sure sounded funny. "Joe has told me so much about you. I don't know how to thank you."

Al started to climb down off the kitchen stool and he sort of fell down the last step. "It was a real pleasure," he said, real polite and everything. He sounded kind of funny too. "I really enjoy trimming a Christmas tree."

What was the matter with him, anyway? He didn't like to trim Christmas trees. "Well, I'll be on my way now," he said. "I'm very glad to have met you."

"Oh, do you have to hurry off?" my mother said. "I'm sure Joe would like you to stay." Boy, her face was sure pink. All of a sudden she didn't look so tired. "I've brought home some fruit cake and I'll just put on some coffee. It won't take but a minute. Won't you sit down?"

My mother sat down in a chair. Al sat down in another chair.

"I understand you work in the post office," my mother said. "That must be interesting work."

"Well, it's only temporary, of course," Al said. "I'm thinking of going back to study architecture. That's the career I'm really interested in, building and all."

What did he say that for? He didn't like building at all. "Hey, Al," I said, "how come . . . ?"

My mother got up and went into the kitchen and started to make some coffee. Pretty soon you could smell the coffee and the Christmas tree all together. It sure smelled good. Al turned on the Christmas tree lights and then he built a fire in the fireplace and then he made the train go. It ran all over the room, under the bridges and over the mountains and through the tunnels. I never saw such a good train.

Pretty soon my mother started to bring in a lot of things to eat, like when we had a party with my father in front of the fire. Her face was all pink, and she kept on smiling and everything. She sure looked nice.

"Do you live around here?" she asked Al.

"Yes, I have a room a few blocks away," Al said. "But before too long I want to build a house with a big yard and plenty of room for a dog and all that."

What did he go and say that for? Boy, he sure must have changed his mind or something.

"Hey, Al," I said. "How come . . . ?"

"Joe," Al said, "there is something I've been meaning to tell you for quite some time."

"What?" I said.

"Merry Christmas," he said.

And that was the night my father came home.

# HOW DOT HEARD *THE MESSIAH*

---

*It used to be that pipe organists could produce no sound without the help of boys who pumped bellows for them behind the scenes. Such a one was young Dot, who had little food to eat but feasted his soul on great church music.*

*And tomorrow there would be no job for him, thus no way of keeping his mother alive. What could he do?*

*This is the oldest story in this collection (more than 120 years old).*

The church was vast and dim. The air was fragrant with pine boughs, and over the golden cross of the chancel hung heavy wreaths of boxwood and fir. A solitary light shone in front of the organ.

Little feet were heard on the stairs leading to the orchestra. A door in the organ case opened quietly and was about to close, when a voice was heard: "Is that you, Dot?"

"Yes, sir."

"What makes you come so early? It is nearly an hour before the rehearsal begins. I should think the little bellows room would be a rather lonely place to wait an hour."

"I always come early," said the boy timidly.

"So I have noticed. Why?"

"Mother thinks it best."

"Come out here, and let me talk with you. I have sung in the choir nearly a year and have hardly had a glimpse of you yet. Don't be bashful! Why, all the music would stop if it were not for you, Dot. Our grandest Christmas anthem would break into confusion if you were to cease to *blow*. Come here. I have just arrived in the city and have come to the church to wait for the hour of rehearsal. I want company. Come, Dot."

The little side door of the organ moved: a shadow crept along in the dim light toward the genial-hearted Tenor.

"Do you like music, Dot?"

"Yes, sir."

"Is that what makes you come so long before the rest?"

"No, sir."

"What is it, then?"

"I have a reason—Mother would not like to have me speak of it."

"Do you sing?"

"Yes, at home."

"What do you sing?"

"The parts I hear you sing."

"Tenor, then?"

"Yes."

"Will you sing for me?"

"Now?"

"Yes."

"I will sing, 'Hark, What Mean?'"

"Rossini—an adaptation from *Cujus Animam.*"

The boy did not understand.

"Well," said the Tenor, "I beat time—now, Dot."

A flute-like voice floated out into the empty edifice, silvery, pure, rising and falling through all the melodious measures of that almost seraphic melody. The Tenor leaped to his feet and stood like one entranced. The voice fell in wavy cadences: "*Heavenly Hallelujahs rise.*" Then it rose clear as a skylark, with the soul of inspiration in it:

> *"Hear them tell that sacred story,*
> *Hear them chant—"*

The Tenor with a nervous motion turned on the gaslight.

The boy seemed affrighted and shrank away toward the little door that led to the bellows room.

"Boy!"

"Sir?"

"There is a fortune in that voice of yours."

"Thank you, sir."

"What makes you hide behind that bench?"

"You won't tell, sir?"

"No: I will befriend any boy with a voice like *that.*"

The boy approached the singer and stood beside him.

He said not a word, but only looked toward his feet.

The Tenor's eyes followed the boy's. He saw it all, but he only said tenderly: "Dot!"

A chancel door opened. An acolyte came in, bearing a long gaslighter: he touched the chandeliers and they burst into flame. The cross glimmered upon the wall under the Christmas wreaths; the alabaster font revealed its beautiful decorations of calla lilies and smilax; the organ glowed with its tall pipes and carvings and cherubs.

The first flash of light in the chancel found Dot hidden in his little room with the door fast closed behind him.

What a strange place it was! A dim light fell through the open carvings of the organ case. Great wooden pipes towered aloft with black mouths—like dragons. Far, far above in the arch was a cherub without a body—a golden face with purple wings. Dot had looked at it for hours and wondered.

He sat looking at it tonight with a sorrowful face. There were other footsteps in the church, sounds of light happy voices.

Presently the bell tinkled. The organist was on his bench. Dot grasped the great wooden handle; it moved up and down, up and down, and then the tall wooden pipes with the dragon mouths began to thunder around him. Then the chorus burst into a glorious strain, which Dot the year before had heard the organist say was the "Midnight Mass of the Middle Ages":

*Adeste fideles*
*Laeti triumphantes,*
*Venite,*
*Venite,*
*In Bethlehem!*

The great pipes close at hand ceased to thunder. The music seemed to run far away into the distance, low, sweet, and shadowy. There were sympathetic solos and tremulous chords. Then the tempest seemed to come back again, and the luminous arch over the organ sent back into the empty church the jubilant chorus:

*Venite adoremus,*
*Venite adoremus,*
*Venite adoremus,*
*Dominum.*

After the anthem there were solos. The Tenor sang one of them, and Dot tried to listen to it as he moved the handle up and down. How sweet it sounded to Dot's ears! It came from a friendly heart—except his mother's it was the only voice that had ever spoken a word of sympathy or praise to the poor bellows boy.

The singers rested, laughed, and talked. Dot listened as usual in his narrow room.

"I came to the church directly from the train," said the Tenor, "and amused myself for a time with Dot. A wonderful voice that boy has."

"Dot?" said the precentor.

"Yes, the boy who blows the organ."

"Oh yes, I had forgotten. I seldom see him," said the precentor. "Now I think of it, the sexton told me some weeks ago that I must get a new organ boy for next year: he says this one—Dot you call him?—comes to the church through back alleys and goes to the bellows room as soon as the church is open and hides there until service time, and that his clothes are not decent to be seen in a church on Sunday. Next Sunday begins the year—I must see to the matter."

"He does his work well?" asked the Alto with a touch of sympathy in her voice.

"Yes."

"Would it not be better to get him some new clothes than to dismiss him?" she asked.

"No. Charity is charity, and business is business. Everything must be first class here. We cannot have ragamuffins creeping into the church to do church work. Of course, I should be glad to have the boy supplied with clothes. That is another thing. But we must have a different person in the bellows box. The sexton's son is bright, dresses well, and I have no doubt would be glad of the place.

"Now we will sing the anthem, '*Good-will to men.*'"

The choir and chorus arose. The organist tinkled the bell and bent down on the pedals and keys. There was a ripple of music, a succession of short sounds, and—silence.

The organist touched the knob at the side of the keyboard and again the bell tinkled. His white hands ran over the keys, but there issued no sound.

He moved nervously from the bench and opened the little door.

"Dot?"

No answer.

"The boy is sick or faint."

The Tenor stepped into the room and brought out a limp figure.

"Are you sick, Dot?"

"Yes, sir; what will become of Mother?"

"He heard what you said about dismissing him," said the Alto to the precentor.

"Yes, but the sexton was right. Look at his shoes—why, his toes are sticking through them."

"And this bitter weather!" said the Alto, feelingly.

"Can you blow, Dot?"

"No, sir; it is all dark, sir. I can't see, sir. I can't but just stand up, sir. You won't dismiss me, sir. Mother is lame and poor, sir—paralyzed, sir: that's what they call it—can't use but one hand, sir."

"This ends the rehearsal," said the precentor in an impatient way. "Dot, you needn't come tomorrow nor till I send for you. Here's a dollar, Dot—charity—Christmas present."

One by one the singers went out, the precentor bidding the sexton have a care that Dot was sent home.

The Alto and the Tenor lingered. Dot was recovering.

"I shall not hear the music tomorrow. I do love it so."

"You poor child, you shall have your Christmas music tomorrow, and the best the city affords. Do you know where Music Hall is, Dot?"

"Yes, lady."

"There is to be an oratorio there tomorrow evening—*The Messiah*. It is the grandest ever composed, and no singing in America is equal to it. There is one chorus called the 'Hallelujah Chorus'—it is wonderful: The man who composed it thought he heard the angels singing and saw the Lord of heaven, when he was at work upon it; and *he* is to be the first tenor singer, and *I* am to sing the alto—wouldn't you like to go, Dot?"

"Yes, lady. Is the man who composed it to be the tenor singer—the one who heard the angels singing, and thought he saw the Lord?"

"No, Dot: *he* is to be the tenor singer."

"*I*, Dot," said the Tenor.

"I have a ticket for the upper gallery, which I will give him," said the Alto. "A friend of mine bought it, but I gave her a seat on the main floor, and kept this for—well, for Dot."

The Tenor talked low with the lady.

"Here is a Christmas present, Dot." He handed Dot a bill.

"And here is one for your mother," said the Alto, giving Dot a little roll of money.

Dot was better now. He looked bewildered at his new fortune.

"Thank you, lady. Thank you, sir. Are you able?"

The Alto laughed. "Yes, Dot. I am to receive a hundred dollars for singing tomorrow evening.* I shall try to think of you, Dot, when I am rendering one of the passages—perhaps it will give me inspiration. I shall see you, Dot—under the statue of Apollo."

The sexton was turning off the lights in the chancel. He called Dot. The church grew dimmer and dimmer, and the great organ faded away in the darkness. In the vanishing lights the Alto and Tenor went out of the church, leaving Dot with the sexton.

*About three thousand dollars in today's money.

❄ ❄ ❄

It was Sabbath evening—Christmas.

Lights glimmered thickly among the snowy trees on the Common; beautiful coaches were rolling through the crowded streets.

Dot entered Music Hall timidly through a long passage through which bright, happy faces were passing, silks rustling, aged people moving sedately and slowly, and into which the crowds on the street seemed surging like a tide. Faces were too eager with expectation to notice *him* or his feet. At last he passed a sharp angle in the long passage, and the great organ under a thousand gas-jets burst upon his view. An usher at one of the many lower doors looked at his ticket doubtfully:

"Second gallery—back."

Dot followed the trailing silks up the broad flights of stairs, reached the top, and asked another usher to show him his seat. The young man whom Dot addressed had that innate refinement of feeling that marks a true Boston gentleman. He gave Dot a smile, as much as to say, "I am glad you can enjoy all this happiness with the rest," and said: "Follow me."

His manner was so kind that Dot thought he would like to speak to him again. He remembered what the Alto had said about the statue of Apollo, and as the usher gave him back his check and pointed to the number on the check and the seat, Dot said: "Will you please tell me, sir, which is the statue of Apollo?"

The usher glanced at the busts and statues along the wall. He spoke kindly: "That is the Apollo Belvedere."

Dot thought that a pretty name; it did not convey

to his mind any association of the Vatican palace, but he knew that some beautiful mystery was connected with it.

And now Dot gazed in amazement on the scene before him. In the blaze of light the great organ rose resplendently, sixty feet in height, its imposing facade hiding from view its six thousand pipes. People were hurrying into the hall, flitting to and fro; young ladies in black silks and velvets and satins; old men—where were so many men with white hair ever seen before? stately men with thin faces, bald—teachers, college professors. Tiers of seats in the form of half a pyramid rose at either end of the organ. These were filling with the chorus—sopranos and altos in black dresses and white shawls, tenors and basses in black coats, white neckties and kids. In front, between the great chorus, rose a dark statue, and around this, musicians were gathering—players with violins, violas, violoncellos, contra basses, flutes, oboes, bassoons, trumpets, trombones, horns; the pyramidal seats filled; the hall overflowed, even the galleries. The instruments tuned. A dark-haired man stepped upon the conductor's stand. He raised his baton; there was a hush, then half a hundred instruments poured forth the symphony.

Dot listened. He had never heard such music before; he did not know that anything like it was ever heard on earth. It grew sweeter and sweeter:

*Comfort ye.*

Did the angel speak? The instruments were sweeter now:

*Comfort ye my people.*

Did that voice come from the air?
Dot listened and wondered if this was earth:

*Comfort ye, comfort ye my people saith your God,*
*saith your God.*

Dot saw a tall man standing alone—in front of the musicians—was it he who was singing? Dot gazed upon his face with wide eyes. It was *he*—and *he* was the Tenor who had befriended him the night before.

What music followed when the chorus arose and sang:

*Every valley shall be exalted!*

Dot heard the grand music sweep on, and he felt, as all felt, that the glorious Messiah was about to appear. He saw a lady in white satin and flashing jewels step forward: he heard a ripple of applause, and a voice full of strength and feeling sang:

*O thou that tellest good tidings to Zion, O thou that tellest good tidings to Jerusalem, say unto the cities of Judah, Behold your God!*

Dot knew that voice. Would indeed she lift her eyes to him?

No, she did not. She sat down, the hall ringing with applause. She rose, bowed, but she did not look towards the statue of Apollo, near which Dot was sitting.

Dot heard dreamy music now, more enchanting than any before it. The great audience did not stir, or move a fan, or raise a glass. It grew more ethereal; it seemed now but a wavy motion in the air. He heard a lady nearby whisper: "The Pastoral Symphony."

The Alto had risen again. She stood out from the great chorus—what a beautiful figure! The dark-haired man lifted his baton: the lady turned her face toward the upper gallery. Her eyes wandered for a moment; they rested on—Dot.

There was no applause now. Tears stood in the Alto's eyes—tears stood in the eyes of every one. There was a deep hush and tears, and in the silence the Alto stood looking steadily at—Dot.

There was a rustle in the hall—it grew. The silence was followed by a commotion that seemed to rock the hall. The applause gathered force like a tempest.

Then the beautiful lady looked toward Dot, and sang again the same wonderful air, and all the hall grew still, and people's eyes were wet again.

"The Hallelujah Chorus" with its grand fugues was sung, the people rising and standing with bowed heads during the majestic outpouring of praise.

❄ ❄ ❄

It is ended now—faded and gone. The great organ stands silent in the dark hall; the coaches have rolled away, the clocks are striking midnight.

"I have come to congratulate you before retiring," said our Tenor to the Alto, as he stepped into the parlor of the Revere House. "Tonight has been the triumph of your life. Nothing so moved the audience as 'He shall feed his flock like a shepherd.'"

"Do you know to what I owed the feeling that so inspired me in that air?"

"No."

"It was poor little Dot in the gallery. You teach music, do you not?"

"Yes."

"You are about to open a school?"

"Yes."

"Give Dot a place as office boy–errand boy–something. It will lift a weight from my heart."

"I had thought of it. He has a beautiful voice. I might get him a place in a choir."

❄ ❄ ❄

Sixteen years have passed. The old Handel and Haydn Society have sung *The Messiah* fifty, perhaps sixty times. The snows of December are again on the hills. The grand oratorio is again rehearsing for the Sabbath evening before Christmas.

A new tenor is to sing on the occasion—he was born in Boston, has studied in Milan, and has achieved great triumphs as an interpreter of sacred music in London and Berlin.

The old hall is filled again. The symphony has begun its dulcet enchantment; the tenor, with a face luminous and spiritual, arises, and with his first notes thrills the audience and holds it as by a spell:

*Comfort ye.*

He thought of the time when he first heard those words. He thought of the hearts whose kindness had made him a singer. Where were they? Their voices had vanished from the choirs of earth, but in spirit those sweet singers seemed hovering around him.

*Comfort ye my people.*

He looked, too, toward the Apollo on the wall. He recalled the limp bellows boy who had sat there sixteen years ago. How those words then comforted him! How he loved to sing them now!

*Speak ye comfortably to Jerusalem, and say unto her that her warfare is accomplished, that her iniquity is pardoned.*

It was Dot.

## *Hezekiah Butterworth*

(1839–1905)

Hezekiah Butterworth was born in Rhode Island. In addition to being editor of one of the greatest youth magazines in American history, *The Youth's Companion* (1870–1894), he also wrote many stories himself, specializing in travel narratives. Among his books are seventeen volumes of *Zigzag Journeys* (1880–1895), *The Story of the Hymns* (1875), *The Great Composers* (1884), and *Brother Jonathan* (1903).

# A CERTAIN STAR

*The renowned scientist discovers that though he may have conquered the most deadly forces in the universe, he is powerless to avert disaster in his own family. Somewhere along the way, he has lost wife, daughter, and son.*

*Will the star help to show him a way back?*

❄ ❄ ❄

*This story was written during the decade after Hiroshima and Nagasaki. The deep insights into what life and death and relationships are all about in this story remind us why Buck was awarded both the Pulitzer Prize and the Nobel Prize. Quite simply, it is one of the most profound Christmas stories ever written.*

He woke at dawn this Christmas morning. For a brief instant he could not remember where he was. Then the warmth of childhood memory crept into his drowsy mind. He was here at the farm, in his old home, the broken rafters of his boyhood room above his head. It was yesterday, only yesterday, that he had insisted upon this homecoming, and against the subdued but massive revolt of his family he had carried it through.

"Oh Dad," his daughter Anne had wailed. "Go to the farm now? On Christmas Eve? But we've planned—"

She had protested with such sparkling anger that he had turned on her with like anger.

"It's been years since I asked anything of you!"

His son spoke. "I have a date, Dad."

"You'll break your date, Hal," he had said firmly.

He had turned then from his two mute and furious children to Helen, his wife.

"Christmas has departed from this house," he told her.

She had smiled patiently. "I'm used to your large announcements, darling. And things are about as they have been, since the war ended. Everything's changed. It's inevitable."

"The foundations don't change," he had insisted. "We must get back to being a family." Then the idea had come. "Pack up, all of you! I'll have the car ready in an hour." He recognized the command in his voice. He had grown used to command during the war, and no less in these years of continuing atomic research. He was accustomed to obedience in his great laboratory of scientists, and he did not stay to hear more protest in his house. And knowing his punctual ways, they had assembled in an hour, and in total silence, for the long drive to the farm.

Well, they had obeyed him, at least. They were here together, miles away from late dancing and much drinking and the time-wasting frivolities that he detested. And it was Christmas. During this day surely he would win them back again. For he had lost them somehow during these years that had been absorbed in his work. His name, his fame, Arnold Welborn, nuclear scientist, one of the top three in the world, had overwhelmed him. Scientists of every country turned to him for advice and argument, and compelled by the rapid growth of knowledge he had dedicated his whole being. This was his duty, of course, during the war, when his experiments in nuclear physics belonged to his government, but the line between duty and the pleasurable excitement of successful work was not so clear after the war ended. While he pursued his separate way, his children had grown up, and Helen was certainly older than she should be. The old joy between them was gone. And yesterday in his own home within easy distance of his laboratory at Columbia, he had suddenly realized that whatever was going on, in spite of last-minute shopping and an artificial modernized tree, it was not Christmas. . . . He remembered Anne, his daughter, so pretty, so feverish, not at all gay, flying to the telephone, always to be disappointed. It was never the right voice. So whose was the voice for which she listened? Oh Anne, beloved child, it was for her sake above all that he wanted to be alone today with his family. . . .

And what of the star? On Christmas mornings, when

he was a boy lying here in this bed, there had been a certain star, high over the barn. He saw it always when he rose, earlier than usual, so that he could get the milking done before they opened the doors to the parlor where the Christmas tree stood. The Christmas star! He threw back the covers and leaped out of bed—nonsense, probably, for the star might not be there now. He was no astronomer and he did not know the ways of a star. Yet as he fumbled in the closet for his old clothes, it occurred to him that in a way the star was responsible for the direction of his life. The star had led him to the heavens.

"What do you want for Christmas, boy?" His father asked the question the year he was fourteen.

"I want a telescope," he had said.

His father had stared at him, his small blue eyes sharp and inquisitive above his ragged beard.

"What for?"

"To look at stars with."

His father had grunted, without sympathy it seemed, but on Christmas morning there was a Sears Roebuck telescope under the tree. It was the only gift he wanted. Impatient for the night, he had been compelled to wait until darkness fell. Then lifting his telescope to his eye, he peered at the star. What disappointment! It was larger, more glowing, but as far off as ever. The next day, in sheer experiment, he had looked at the sun, and to his astonishment he saw spots upon it, and this had led to the buying of a book, an introduction to the sky, and so had begun his interest in cosmic rays.

He was dressed now in ski pants, leather jacket, and fur boots. He slammed the door as he left the room, then winced, for Helen was still asleep, he hoped. If he had waked her, she would be patient with him, as indeed she had always been ever since his dark prowlings, begun long ago because his famous hunches, coming by night as well as by day, made it necessary for him to sleep alone. He could bear no interruption when he was seized by a theory, and knew no peace until he had pursued it.

"When you marry me," he told Helen the day they were engaged, "you don't marry a man. You marry a sort of—of monster."

She had only laughed. Then one day during the war, when they were living in a barracks at Los Alamos, she had looked at him thoughtfully.

"What does that look mean?" he had inquired.

"Perhaps you *are* a sort of monster," she had said.

He had laughed, but the words came back to him now as he stepped outside the kitchen door into the darkness. The cold was solid enough to cut, the colder because the house was warm. He had put in an oil burner years ago when the children were small, but when he was a boy there had been only the huge wood range in the kitchen. It was still there, for memory's sake. . . .

The snow creaked under his boots as he walked toward the barn. The sky was clear, the stars luminous and twinkling through the icy air. He looked up, searching the heavens. Ah, his star was plain! There it hung over the ridgepole of the barn, not so large as he had imagined, but unmistakably the same. The years had painted it bigger and more golden than it was now, or perhaps his boy's imagination had seen it so. Yet there it shone, steady and true, as he had remembered it.

His feet found the familiar groove in the path under the snow, and as he stood in the windless air, the old wonder came flooding back again, the wonder of the universe. He had known it years ago, distilled through the single star. He had lost it in the hurry and excitement of his youth, in the years when he had been working for a living by day in the laboratory of a great industry. In his own small laboratory by night, he had explored the secrets of the explosive rays of the sun, and using his meager holidays he had sought Einstein in Germany and Rutherford in England. Skeptic and daring, he had wandered far from this humble place upon which he stood to gaze again at a star on Christmas morning. He had been a proud and argumentative man, until the day when he had found terror and a new humility in the nucleus of an atom, laid bare before him in a hidden place in the desert. Infinite energy, encased in a shape so small that eye could not see it! Yes, this star upon which he now gazed had guided his life. What next? Where would the path lie from this Christmas morning?

He shivered suddenly and remembered that he was standing halfway to his knees in snow. It had fallen during the night, the soft stuff clinging to every branch and twig, and the air from the lake was icy. He turned reluctantly and followed his own tracks back to the house and into the kitchen.

The light was on when he opened the door and Helen, wrapped in her red flannel bathrobe, was standing at the gas stove, making coffee.

"Merry Christmas," he said and kissed her cheek. "Did I wake you?"

"You're as cold as a snowman," she said, rubbing that cheek. "And you didn't wake me. I couldn't sleep."

"Christmas in your bones?"

She shook her head. "I don't sleep as well as I used to." She set two cups on the table and poured the coffee. "You want breakfast now?"

"No, but I'll have coffee."

They sat down. She sipped her coffee slowly, but he took a hot gulp.

"That's good—I was cold all the way through."

"What were you doing outside at this hour?" she asked.

"What would you say if I told you I went out to see a star?" he replied.

"It's been a long time since you were interested in stars," she said.

He glanced at her. She looked too tired, this slender wife of his. "Maybe we shouldn't have come here to the farm. Maybe it's too much for you. Don't you feel well, Helen?"

"I'm all right," she said. "Just getting old, I suppose."

She got up to make more coffee. "I heard Anne crying in the night."

He stared at her in consternation. "Why should Anne cry?"

"They don't say anything," she told him. "You know they never say anything nowadays. One doesn't know what goes on in anybody."

She threw him a strange sad look which he did not comprehend.

"Anne seemed perfectly willing to come here yesterday," he reminded her. "She was more willing than Hal was—he had a dance or something."

"They both had parties." She stirred her coffee thoughtfully. "It isn't like Anne to give up so easily—not if she wants something."

"That's true."

Anne never gave up easily when she wanted something very much. So yesterday obviously there wasn't anything she wanted very much.

"I hope she wants the bracelet I've bought her for Christmas," he grumbled. "It cost enough."

"I don't know what they want anymore. Everybody's changed somehow." She sighed and began sipping her coffee again, holding her cup in both hands as though they were cold.

He examined her face, still so pretty in spite of pallor. It had been a long time since he had seen her in the morning before she made up her face. He was an early worker, and she slept late.

"Are you all right?" he asked again.

"Tired," she said. "My time of life, maybe."

"Woman's retreat," he declared. He got up and kissed her cheek. "Remember how you used to climb Mont Blanc with me when we were measuring cosmic rays? That wasn't so long ago."

She smiled faintly and did not reply. He tousled her hair to tease her and she caught his hand and slapped it gently. "I'll bet that your Christmas presents aren't wrapped."

"You're wrong! I had them wrapped at Tiffany's," he said.

She looked shocked. "Did you get everything there?"

"Everything," he said, "and when I said I wanted them gift wrapped, the clerk said stiffly that the usual Tiffany wrapping *was* a gift wrapping."

That made her laugh, and he felt victorious.

"And now," he said, "I am going upstairs to the attic to bring down my precious parcels for the tree."

"Why on earth did you take them to the attic?" she inquired. "The children won't snoop—you forget they're grown."

"Habit. Before I knew it last night I was in the attic, putting my small expensive packages in the corner where we hid Anne's dollhouse and Hal's bicycle. . . . How many years has it been since we spent Christmas here?"

"Not since you busied yourself with the nucleus of an atom," she said. There was a glint of old mischief in her blue eyes. "I wish I knew the enchantment in a nucleus!"

"Ah, there's enchantment," he retorted. He left her then and climbed the stairs to the attic and found his gifts in the brown paper bag in which he had thrust them for safekeeping yesterday. Halfway down the stairs again to the second floor he heard Anne's voice in the upper hall as she talked to someone—a man, of course!

"What's the use of my coming into town tonight? . . . Yes, I could come with Hal—he's got a date—but what's the use? It would be midnight before you could get away from your family and we'd have fifteen minutes—well, half an hour then—and you uneasy all the time! What good is that?"

He heard the passion and the pain and, his heart suddenly aching, he saw her there at the telephone. She was still in her pink flannel nightgown, her yellow hair curling over her shoulders, a mere child in spite of her twenty years. No man had the right to hurt this child he had begotten! How could he persuade her to tell his name so that he could defend her from the fellow?

"Anne," he said.

She hung up instantly. Then she turned and looked up at him with huge startled blue eyes.

"It's early for you to be up on Christmas morning, isn't it?" he asked.

"I couldn't sleep," she said. "It's terribly cold here by the lake."

"It's just as well you're up," he said. "We have the tree to cut, Hal and I, and we'll trim it and get dinner together the way we used to do. I'll bring in some branches for you to decorate the house with—maybe some ground pine, eh?"

He deposited the brown bag on the stairs and came toward her.

"Feeling sentimental, aren't you, Santa Claus?" She crossed the hall to meet him and standing tiptoe she kissed his cheek. "You're a sweet old thing," she said suddenly.

"Thank you," he said. "I haven't heard even that for a long time."

"I haven't said anything to you for a long time," she agreed. "You've been away somewhere these ten years, haven't you?"

She was tracing the outline of his eyebrow with a delicate forefinger.

"It's you," he said, capturing the forefinger. "You've

grown up without asking me. I get only glimpses of the daughter I used to have."

All the same, he was thinking, if he hadn't insisted on being here today there wouldn't have been even this interchange. She'd have been asleep in her bed, exhausted by dancing and carryings on. She leaned her head against his breast unexpectedly.

"I wish I were little again," she whispered. "I wish I had never grown up!"

He pressed her soft hair. "Why, Anne—why, Anne—"

"Silly, isn't it!" She lifted her head and shook the tears from eyes that smiled up at him too brightly. Then running to her room she shut the door against him.

"Merry Christmas," he called after her, but she did not answer.

He opened Hal's door then. There, sprawled across the bed, lay his dear and only son—eighteen, a six footer, handsome, brilliant—and a total stranger! He tiptoed across the floor and looked down at his sleeping child. A man, this child—a child, this man! Tall, thin with youth, big bones, fresh skin, and dark hair too long, here was his son, holding within the new shape of manhood a thousand memories of boyhood. Hal it used to be who could not wait to get to the lake in summer, to swim, to fish, to boat. Twice he was nearly drowned in the deep still waters, the first time swimming beyond his strength, the second time by a blow on the head against a rock when he dived. Twice he was saved, both times by himself, the father. Three times, then, this son had been given to him alive, the first time fresh from his mother's womb.

Now he was a stranger who drove wildly into the

night, who danced obscene dances with persons unknown, who came home, sometimes drunk, to break the hearts of his parents. How could his son be saved? For inside that noble skull there was a brain worth saving. His own old professor at Harvard had written him about Hal. "If you can pull him through this pretentious youthfulness, this cult of beat, you'll have a man."

Suddenly Hal opened his eyes and looked at him.

"What do you want, Dad?"

"Merry Christmas," he said.

Hal yawned. "Is it time to get up?"

"We have the tree to cut after breakfast."

Hal turned and burrowed into his pillow. "Okay—okay—"

Arnold stood an instant longer, stifling his sudden impatience. Christmas, and the boy wanted to sleep! He remembered other mornings when Hal came into his room at dawn, shouting for the day to begin. And he had cut short his own sleep and had gotten out of bed so that his son could be happy. He turned abruptly and left the room, closing the door just short of a bang. Patience! He was exhausted with being patient. Hal had no self-discipline. Why did men have children?

He went into his own room and stood by the window. The snow was falling again in a flurry from a sky overcast with gray clouds. The star was gone.

The sky was clear again when he and Hal went tramping through the snow after breakfast. His spirits rose in spite of himself. Filled with warm and nourishing food, encouraged by the sight of a pretty flush on Helen's cheeks, though it might be no more than the heat of the old wood range, which he had insisted upon lighting in honor of the day, and softened by Anne's sporadic tenderness, he inclined his heart anew to this tall and silent youth who was his son.

"When I was a kid," he said, "we always had a white Christmas. We took it for granted. And I believe that you and Anne always took snow for granted, too, in the years when we came here for your Christmas holidays. Snow isn't so important in the city."

Behind him he heard Hal's crunching tread, but there was no answer to his small talk. He glanced over his shoulder, breathing out his frosty breath, and saw Hal's blank face. The boy was not listening. Then he caught his father's sharp glance.

"Did you say something, Dad?"

"Nothing important," he said shortly.

They tramped on. Why talk to a son who heard nothing? And he had a great deal to say to a son, a very great deal. He longed to share with Hal something of his own life, the excitement of being a scientist in the atomic age when a scientist had suddenly become the most important man in the world. Once, isolated in his laboratory, working alone, experimenting haphazardly often, and usually in vain, a scientist had been scarcely human, a magician to fear. Now, with the knowledge of the energy that was in the core of the universe, that infinitely small core, he was the man of the future. . . . Did Hal dream of such things? There was no way of knowing, no communication possible between father and son.

He paused to examine the spruce woods in which they stood. The trees had grown too tall. They would have to look for young growth beyond.

"How far are you going?" Hal demanded.

"We must find a tree of reasonable size," he said. "We'll go to the edge of the forest."

"We could cut the top out of any tree," Hal said.

He shook his head. "I'm too good a woodsman for that. My father's ghost would rise. Kill a whole tree for its top?"

"It's getting late," Hal urged.

"What's your hurry?" he demanded.

Hal stopped in the snow. "Dad, I want to get back to town by eight o'clock tonight."

He turned and faced his son. "Well, you can't! One thing I asked of my family this Christmas—the gift I really want—that we spend the day together here. And the day includes the evening. It will be six o'clock before we get dinner over. Then we'll have the tree."

He saw a strange look in Hal's eyes, a muted rebellion. If the boy felt that way, why didn't he fling out his anger? Once when he himself was eighteen, he had fought his father first with words, and then with fists. It had concerned a day, too, a summer's day when he had wanted to go to the state fair, and his father had forbidden it.

"Hay's fit to cut," his father had said roughly. "Nobody ain't goin' nowheres."

"I'm going," he had said.

"Try it!" his father had shouted.

They had glared at each other. Suddenly his father had bellowed at him. "If you feel like you look, we'll fight it out—see who's the better man—"

They had fought, wrestling like bulls, young and old, and he had downed his father. He had watched his father get to his feet, pride and shame tearing his heart in two.

"All right," his father had said sullenly. "I'll make hay alone."

"I'm not going," he said, and the two of them had worked side by side throughout the long hot hours until sunset. . . . Yes, that boy who had been himself he could understand. Why didn't Hal defy him?

"You're the boss," Hal said. "Guess you'll always be the boss now—and you know it."

He stared at his son's bitter face. "What do you mean by that?"

"Just what I said. You're the boss! You've been the big boss ever since the war, haven't you? Atomic bomb master!"

He stared at the dark young giant, who glowered at him. Then rage ran over his body like fire and he hit his son on the jaw, a clean right-hander that amazed him. In the same instant he recognized pride in the blow—a low male pride that horrified him. His hand dropped.

"Hal!" he stammered. "Hal, I didn't mean—I don't know what got into me. But you called me a vile name. Still, I shouldn't have done it."

Hal pulled his handkerchief out of his pocket and mopped his face.

"Is it bleeding?" he asked casually.

"Yes, a little. It's a bad bruise. . . . What made you call me that name, boy?"

"It's what you are, aren't you? A sort of master scientist—"

"No!"

Hal inspected the handkerchief, spattered with blood. He rolled it up and put it back in his pocket.

"Okay. . . . Let's cut the Christmas tree."

"Hal, I can't just let this pass."

"I said okay—okay."

"Okay, then!"

He was furious again and he stalked grimly ahead of his son for fifty paces. Then he stopped before a young spruce.

"Here's our tree," he said.

"I'll cut it," Hal said.

He swung the axe three times against the trunk, each time missing the groove. Then he threw down the axe.

"I'm dizzy, Dad."

"Let me look at your face." He cupped his hand under his son's chin and examined the blackening bruise. "I'll ask you to forgive me for such an act on Christmas Day," he said abruptly.

"It's all right," Hal said. "I called you a name."

"Which I don't deserve," he maintained. "But rest yourself—I'll chop down the tree."

He struck four clean blows and the tree fell away with a long groan. He lifted the stump end and Hal took the top and in silence they carried it down their tracks and across the meadow to the front porch of the house.

"I'll brush the snow off," Hal said.

"Let's go into the house and get warm first."

He led the way into the kitchen. The room was warm and fragrant with sage and roasting turkey.

"Hi there, you two," Helen called cheerfully. She

was basting the bird in the oven, her face rosy and her hair a tumble of silvery curls.

"There's no oven like this one," she went on. "I wonder that we were ever willing to give up wood ranges."

"Wait until you have an atomic oven," he retorted. "A couple of minutes and your turkey is done. We sit down to the table and you press a button. We exchange a little small talk, pass the time of day, and the bird will be ready to carve."

Nobody answered. He was pulling off his boots and did not notice the silence. At the kitchen table Anne was polishing the old farmhouse silver.

"Any telephone calls?" Hal asked.

"None," Anne said. She looked up and gave a cry. "What's the matter with your face?"

"Your face," Helen echoed. She closed the oven door. "Why, it's awful!"

"I hit Hal," Arnold said harshly. He got up and drew a glass of water and drank it.

"I called Dad a name," Hal said.

Helen sat down on the kitchen stool. "Oh dear, oh dear—what is the matter with us—"

"Christmas gift!" Anne said, and shrieking with laughter she buried her face in her hands.

"Anne!" Arnold shouted. "Stop it! Stop laughing. Stop it, I tell you—"

He seized her shoulders and shook her. She lifted her face to him, broken with laughter or weeping, he did not know which.

"Are you going to hit me, too, Dad? Is that the sort of man you are now?"

He stepped back. "What do you mean?" he demanded. He looked from one face to the other. "What do any of you mean?"

It was Anne who answered. She was the fierce one, the little fierce one who flew at him and bit him one day when she was seven, and in all justice he had been compelled to spank her for unprecedented naughtiness because she had drawn pictures of lambs and daisies over his sheets of formulas. The scars of her little teeth were on his thumb still.

"We don't know you," Anne said distinctly. "You're changed. You've become a stranger to us."

He contemplated these three whom he loved. For a moment he felt helpless and driven to escape. He thought of flight—anywhere to get away from them. Why had he ever left the comfort of his laboratory? Yet he could not escape them, wherever he was. He loved them, each of them differently and all too well. Wherever he went he carried them with him because he loved them. . . . And now he must face them as he had faced the other terrifying decisions of a scientist's life. Should he pursue this knowledge to the uttermost, too, as he had pursued the quest of the energy locked in the nucleus of the atom? There had been times when he longed to escape that ultimate knowledge, yet he had been stern with himself. There could be no escape for the scientist. Even while he knew that a secret energy could and might destroy the world, he had pursued the knowledge of it as his duty. It could, rightly used, heat and light the homes and factories of the world, and so bring life instead of death. In a strange way love was like that, a power for evil or for good. Everything depended upon the human being. So why were these three strangers to him now when he loved them so much? On this Christmas morning, he was conscious only of love. How could he make them understand?

He sat down at the kitchen table and looked from one face to the other. They were watching him and he made himself gentle before them.

"Anne," he said at last, choosing her face among the three. "You're as honest as the Christmas star. I appreciate it. You've made me see myself in a new light. It makes me wonder what I really am. You say I'm a stranger to you, my family. . . . And all the time I've been thinking that you were the strangers—you and Hal, and even you, Helen. I've felt lost here. But I've felt lost for a long time—in my own house."

Anne was embarrassed. He saw it. He must take it more slowly. "You've been busy, Dad—" she said.

"I've been busy, of course," he agreed. "Too much away from you all, too busy about what I thought was my duty—and my job—as it is. A scientist has a peculiar obligation to the age in which he is born. But I can't live without you, my—my dears, whatever I am."

He yearned for their understanding but, searching their faces, he saw them still wary. . . . They didn't know him as he was now. Other memories crowded their minds. He'd tell them he loved them, try to win them back again, prove that he was still the happy and tender father, the passionate lover and husband. But he wouldn't plead. He spoke to Anne again.

"Go on being honest. Why do you feel I am a stranger?"

Her lovely little face set in a defensive terror. "People

ask me how it feels to have a father who—who made the atomic bomb. They ask me what you're making now. And I say I don't know. Because I don't. You never tell us anything."

Hal broke in. "Don't blame Dad for the bomb! Whatever he had to do about that, he had to do it. Besides, it is all over—long ago."

"But to drop it," Anne whispered, staring at him. "How could you let that happen—and on people! That's what they ask me. Why didn't he drop it on an empty island, that's what they say. And I can't answer them."

Hal defended him again, men against women. "He had to be willing for it to be used, the way it was meant to be used . . . to stop the war."

Helen spoke too quietly. "But did it stop the war?"

He spoke in his own defense now, throwing a grateful glance at his son. "My darling, it did. . . . I had the information, then very secret, that the invasion of Japan was planned for a certain date. It was estimated, conservatively, that half a million Americans must die in the invasion, and at least two-and-a-half million Japanese. Against that minimum I had to balance a quarter of a million people in one Japanese city."

"But if you had dropped it on an empty island—"

He was impatient with the old argument, and he compelled himself to patience. Long ago he should have made his explanations. But he had trusted blindly to their love, to their faith in him . . . and love and faith were not enough.

He spoke sternly. "We had only one bomb and no time for experiments, the Nazis being so nearly ready with a bomb to drop upon us. Suppose we had dropped the one bomb we had and it was a dud—"

"You dropped two," Anne said coldly.

"Because the militarists in control of Japan were not willing to surrender, even on the Emperor's order. The second bomb made surrender possible—with honor. Nobody knew how many more bombs we had. . . ."

He stared at them, transfixed with dismay.

"Goodness, have you been hating me ever since the bombs were dropped, you three?"

"Not hating you," Helen said softly. "Just not—knowing you."

"Not knowing what you would do next," Anne said. "That's what people say. What will men like you do next? You have your own secrets and the rest of us don't know what you're thinking or planning."

"And so you don't trust me," he said gravely.

"How can we?" his daughter asked simply. "We don't know what you know. We don't know what you are."

He held his head in his hands then, in deep thought. In the big warm kitchen the delicious smells of pine branch and roasting turkey combined. Outside the day had changed. The sky was darkening and snow was beginning to fall again in the windless air, great soft flakes. To the outer eye it was a Christmas scene as traditional as the turkey in the oven, the spruce tree waiting on the front porch. He remembered it the same on every Christmas of his childhood, and yet today there was something in this house that had never been here before. A fear had unfolded itself, a human fear of a future possible and hideous because of what he and his fellow scientists had done. He had become a monster in his own house.

And if the fear were here, was it not in every other house, in every other heart, a secret unspoken, a shadow unexplained? He who had discovered a miracle had failed to share it with these he loved. They knew only the fear. And the fear they had kept from him, because they wanted to believe in him—and love him—although as Anne said, they no longer knew what he was. Yet if they wanted to love him, then he had not lost them altogether!

He lifted his head. "Let me try," he said. "Let me try to explain myself. I think I understand why you are afraid of me."

Anne could not bear this. "Dad, not afraid of you, exactly! Afraid that something has been let loose in the world that even you can't control. Nobody feels safe anymore. That's why we rush around—we don't dare to think about it. None of us do. So we just keep rushing around, not thinking."

His wife took pity. "I know you can't help it, Arnold. It's got beyond you."

Hal flung himself at them impatiently. "We fellows don't give a rip about this, Dad. What's got to be, will be. There's nothing that anybody can do about it now. I guess people have always been afraid of what's new. Cave men were scared of fire, I guess. We're on our way—might as well cheer up and have a good time—right, Dad?"

He listened to them while they brought the world into this house on Christmas Day. Yes, here was the fear that rotted the heart and destroyed the joy of life.

"I have a fear, too," he said at last. "The fear you have is a fear I share."

They stopped talking. They were listening to him as they had not listened before. He was saying something new.

"Are you afraid of yourself?" Anne asked.

"No," he said strongly. "I know myself. Yes, I am changed, but not as you think. No one can explore the infinite as I have explored it and not come back changed. I am a humble man as I was never humble before. I believe in God. . . ."

He spoke the words simply, aware of their tremendous significance. He had never spoken the Name before. Agnostic and skeptic, he had taken pride in disbelief.

"Not the God of my fathers, perhaps," he went on, trying to be plain and not sentimental, "but, yes, I believe in the eternal Creator, maker of heaven and earth. . . . How can I not believe? I have seen creation at work in the center of the atom—purposive and, though invisible to the eye, immeasurable in its power and its energy. . . . I believe where I cannot see."

They were so still that they seemed not to breathe while he laid his soul bare. It occurred to him now that he had never spoken to them of his serious thoughts. The days of their years together had skimmed by upon the surface of life. He had been too shy, perhaps, to uncover the hidden realities. And they had starved for reality. They were relaxing, listening, Anne on the floor, her hands clasped about her drawn-up knees, Hal leaning against the door, hands in his pockets, and Helen sitting at the table, her head bent. She was listening, he knew, but skeptically, perhaps. Perhaps they were all skeptical!

He faltered. He tried to laugh. "Sounds big, doesn't it? Maybe I'm fooling myself. A man can't live through the years I've had without being changed in ways he himself may not understand."

"I must baste the turkey again," Helen said suddenly.

He suspected, from the look on her too-sensitive face, that the moment was more than she could bear. They watched while she dipped the fat juice with a big spoon and poured it over the huge and supine bird. In these ways, he thought, were the vast, the small, mingled in their lives today. Christmas star and atomic fears!

She drew a glass of cold water, drank it, and sat down again at the table.

"Go on, Dad," Anne said.

"I don't know how to go on now," he said abruptly. "It's true I've been away for years. Even though I sleep and eat at home a good deal of the time—I'm somewhere else. Wandering in the universe, I suppose you'd call it. Maybe I can't get back. Maybe we'll never really meet again, you three and I. A scientist is the loneliest man in the world. We don't make contact except with each other, in our own world. That's why we keep going to conferences and meetings, I suppose—trying to find people who speak our language—with whom we can communicate through our formulas. . . . You've got to meet me halfway, you three!"

"Suppose we can't," Anne said in a low voice.

"Then I suppose I'll have to go my way alone," he said somberly.

Helen got up and went to the window and stood there watching the drifting snow. "We're all in the atomic age together," she said. "You got there first, that's all."

"That's very perceptive of you, darling," he said gratefully.

The telephone rang. Hal went into the hall to answer it and they waited.

"I don't know whether I'm coming," they heard him say. "I won't know for a while yet. . . . I'll be late if I do come—plenty late."

He came back. He threw himself down on the shaggy rug before the kitchen range, crossed his hands under his head, and stared at the ceiling.

"Go on, Pop," he said. "This is getting interesting."

"I can't go on," he said to his son. "You'll have to take me on faith. You can believe in me whatever I do, or you can't believe in me. All I can say is that I have seen a vision as truly as the wise men of old who followed the star to find a newborn child. They believed that the child would bring in a new and better age . . . and so do I."

"Plenty of people were afraid of that new age, too," Helen said.

"Right again," he said and again was grateful.

She had been peering out of the window, and now she went to the breadbox and found a crust and crumbled it. Then she opened the window and put the crumbs on the outside sill.

"I see a belated wood thrush," she said.

"Herod tried to kill the child, remember?" This was Anne, remembering the old story.

He turned to her. "He wanted to stop the new age and he failed. Nobody can stop the coming of a new age—nobody and nothing. There's no going back to what we were. . . . Herod couldn't kill the child . . . and we can't destroy the creative nucleus of the atom. It's eternal. It's there. We have to learn how to use it—for good and only for good."

He got to his feet restlessly and began pacing the floor, from the window to the south, from the window to the north, while the snow drove white against the panes. The big old kitchen stretched the width of the solid house. And he mused aloud.

"I wish it could have begun differently—in peace instead of in war. I wish I could have lighted cities and made houses warm and perfected a fuel for wonderful machines that aren't even invented yet. . . . But it couldn't begin that way, it seems. We had first of all to stop a subhuman man from destroying the world."

He paused and faced them.

"You understand? Hitler would have destroyed us! We were only months ahead."

"But Germany had surrendered," Anne said.

"Japan hadn't," he retorted. "And there were subhumans there who wanted to keep on fighting. It's the subhumans we have to watch."*

He was pacing the floor again. "The only thing I fear in life is the subhuman. I trust the energy in the atom—you can know it and learn to use it—it's predictable.

*In both world wars, American thought-leaders and propagandists used the word *subhuman* to stir up hatred against the German and Japanese peoples. Once they were perceived as such, killing them by the millions did not seem like such an evil act.

And I trust a good man as I trust God. But the subhuman—no! He's the enemy—the only one we have. And he may live next door as well as across the sea. He might be alive in one of us—even in me!"

He stopped in front of Anne and jabbed his long forefinger at her. "That's why you're afraid of me!"

His hand dropped. "Child—you *should* be afraid of me! I was afraid of myself this morning." He turned to Hal. "Son, why did I hit you? I love you. . . . So why did I hit you?"

"Forget it," Hal said under his breath. "I was mad at you, too."

"I can't forget," his father said. "I'll never forget it. I'll have to watch myself. . . . There's something subhuman, even in me."

He had forgotten them in the horror of his discovery. He was talking aloud to himself, to anybody, to everybody. He was putting his soul into words this Christmas morning. But they listened. Even though it was too much for them, they knew what he was talking about. Helen held out her hand to him and he grasped it. Anne laid her forehead against her hunched knees and he saw her body tremble. Was she weeping? He did not know. He had laid himself bare. Let them accept him or reject him.

Hal leaped up from the floor and clapped him on the back. "Enough talk! I guess we understand each other better, anyway. Let's get the tree up, Dad. I'll drag it into the living room through the front door."

"I'll find the Christmas-tree trimmings," Helen said. She stopped on her way and kissed his cheek. But Anne sat crouched on the floor, her head bent. He glanced at her and went to the window and looked out. The snow had ceased to fall, and between the wintry gray of the sky he saw lines of blue again. A variable sort of day, he thought, and it was not half over. Getting up early, even to see a star, was beginning to tell on him. And all this commotion in his family—who knew how deep it went? He had lost too much time to retrieve in one day. And yet not for years with them or anyone else would he have missed the solemn wonders of his laboratory. If he must lack the closeness of family love, he shared a mystery with his fellow scientists. Perhaps that was more than love. A man could not have everything in one life. Perhaps he was born to live alone.

And then Anne lifted her head and began to talk. "I've wanted for weeks to tell you . . . I'm terribly unhappy."

He felt his heart leap. Then he had not utterly failed!

"Tell me why you're unhappy, Anne."

"I've fallen in love."

He drew up the hassock and sat down within reach if she put out her hand to him.

"But that's wonderful," he said gently.

"It's not," she said. "I love someone who doesn't love me."

"Not possible," he declared. "I don't believe there's a man on earth who can't love you, even if he's blind and can't see the way you look."

She laughed brokenly and scrambled to her feet. She came to him and leaned her cheek on top of his head so that he could not see her face.

"He doesn't love me though," she said. "Not enough

to give up anything for me—only enough to kiss me and—and so on."

"And so on," he repeated. "That's not enough. I agree."

"No," she said. "Because I love him too much. So it's got to be everything or nothing. . . . Dad, he's married. So it's nothing."

"That's bleak," he agreed gravely. "That's very bleak."

She broke at his tenderness. "Oh Dad, the world's empty!"

He pulled her to his knees, a child again as she used to be and a child still. She buried her face against his shoulder and began to weep soundlessly, as a broken heart must weep. No, she was not a child. A child sobs aloud. . . . He held her, waiting. He could not throw out the usual snips and bits of comfort. You are only twenty—there are other men, young and handsome. This will pass, my child, this will pass. He would speak only the truth.

She lifted her distraught face. "Shall I ever get over this, Dad?"

"Never," he said. "One never gets over these big things. They stay in you. Other things will come—other loves. You'll live in them, too. You'll live in everything. We must—there's no escape from living."

Her head drooped to his shoulder again, but she was not weeping now. He felt the heart in agony but her mind was working, her will assembling itself. She sat up and smoothed her hair.

"What would have happened to me if you hadn't made us come here for Christmas?" she asked.

"Tell me," he said.

"I planned to run away—with him for a weekend. And this morning I couldn't. I heard you get up and go outside. I went to the window and watched you tramp through the snow and stand there by the barn a long time."

"I had to see the star again," he said.

"The star?"

He told her then of what the Christmas star had meant to the child that he had once been, here in this old house, and how yesterday in the city he had longed intolerably to come back, to get his bearings again by the star.

She slipped from his knees, no more the child. "That's what I need—to get my bearings."

"Sense of proportion," he said. "What's important and what isn't."

She walked to the window as he spoke and now she, too, stood looking out upon the snowy scene.

"Don't tell anyone about me, Dad—"

He was horrified. "How can you think I would?"

"I thought you might say something to Mother."

"You haven't?"

"No. She has enough to worry her."

"Something I don't know?"

"She thinks nobody knows. The doctor told me."

He went cold. "I should have been told at once, Anne."

"She didn't want you told, especially none of us until after Christmas. That's why he told me. Somebody ought to know, he said."

"She doesn't want me told," he repeated, stupefied. "But the doctor ought not to have listened to her!"

"She wouldn't even let him give her the tests until after Christmas. That's why he told me—in case she didn't feel well meanwhile."

He groaned. "All these doors shut between us!"

She came back to him and put out her hand and he clasped it for comfort. "You've opened one door today, Dad—to yourself. And one open door helps the rest of us. We can communicate."

"Will you?"

"I will—I promise."

She smiled at him a wise and sad smile. Some of the brightness of youth was already gone from her face.

"You'll be all right," he said. "Not at once, but step by step, a day at a time."

"Yes . . ."

She paused and sniffed. "Dad—the turkey!"

She flew to the oven, and he grinned and went away. Out in the hall he called. "Helen, where are you?"

From afar off, from behind a closed door her voice answered indistinctly.

"She's upstairs," Hal said from the living room.

The tree was up and fastened in its stand, and he was pounding a last nail. "She went up to get the tree decorations and she hasn't come down. Maybe she can't find the silver star for the top. She couldn't remember where she put it."

He did not wait for Hal to finish. Up the stairs he leaped and to her door. It was locked. He tried the handle.

"Let me in, Helen!"

"Just a minute, dear."

Her voice came faintly through the panels, but in less than a minute she turned the key and opened the door. She did look faint. Her eyes were enormous in her white face.

"Darling, what is the matter?" he cried.

He took her in his arms and she clung to him without answer.

"Why did you come up here all by yourself and lock the door?" he demanded.

"I don't want to tell you," she whispered. "I don't want to spoil our Christmas."

"It's a day for telling," he said. "It's a day for trust."

"I'm not well," she faltered. "Something is wrong with me."

He looked down at the beloved face, pressed against his breast. The eyes were closed.

"Why didn't you tell me?"

"I couldn't—you were so far away."

"You went to the doctor all by yourself."

"Yes." The word was a sigh.

"What did he say?"

"The tests aren't complete."

"Am I far away now?"

"No."

"Never again?"

"Never."

"I'm going with you to the doctor tomorrow—and I'm staying with you."

She lifted a face suddenly bright. "Oh Arnold, will you?"

"And maybe nothing is wrong," he said, "nothing that can't be mended."

"I can believe it possible—now."

She looked up at him, in her eyes a trust renewed. He bent his head and kissed her with a passion deeper than he had known in years. They were close again.

Downstairs Hal was telephoning.

"Hi, kid! Say, I can't get there tonight. . . . No, not even late. . . . I'm just not coming, see? . . . We're having our tree and everything."

The receiver slammed and he yelled up the stairs. "Dad—Mom—you two up there? Are you bringing the Christmas stuff down? And don't forget the star!"

They drew apart and smiled. It was impossible not to hope on this Christmas day. That indeed was the whole meaning of the star.

"Coming, Son," he called. "And we won't forget the star."

## Pearl S. Buck

(1892–1973)

Pearl S. Buck towers over twentieth century American literature, being one of the few people who was awarded both the Pulitzer Prize and the Nobel Prize for Literature. Born in Hillsboro, West Virginia, she spent much of her early life in China with her missionary parents. Her best sellers include *The Good Earth* (1931), *Dragon Seed* (1942), and *Imperial Woman* (1956).

# SEASON OF UNCERTAINTY

---

*Carl could not face Christmas as usual this year—not without Uncle Rich. In fact, without him, thirteen-year-old Carl was afraid.*

*Afraid of those telephone calls.*

"More stuffing, Carl?"

"No thanks."

"Come on, Carl. You haven't eaten your usual six helpings yet."

"I said no *thanks*."

A second of silence passed before Aunt Karen pointed the plate at my grandfather, and I chewed on my lip. I didn't look in my father's direction. I promised him I'd be civil at the table—and I would've been, if they'd all left me alone.

But ever since Gramps had said "Amen" it had been, "So, Carl, you're awfully quiet these days," and "Carl, where's that appetite?" and "Smile, Pal. It can't be that tough."

None of them—Aunt Karen, Uncle Bryan, Gramps, or Grandma—had seen me since Uncle Rich's funeral. They didn't know that it was still "that tough," and that I wasn't the same, in appetite or smile or anything else.

But that wasn't what really made me snap. They seemed to have gotten on with their lives. Not one of them felt the hole Uncle Rich had left behind like I did.

"You made enough mashed potatoes, Maggie," Aunt Karen had said to my mother.

"I was thinking of Rich, I guess," Mom had said. "I miss him today."

"But if he were here, he'd still be suffering, and none of us wants that, right?"

"Right," they'd all agreed.

I didn't want him suffering either. I just wanted him here—before the cancer. Before the chemotherapy. Before he died and left me with so many things unsolved.

My grandfather chuckled now. "Do you know what I miss about Rich? Every Christmas he'd say he forgot film for his camera just as we were sitting down at the table. I'd always say, 'I'll get you some from my bag.' And when I came back he'd say, 'Sorry, Dad. The sweet potatoes are gone.'" Gramps rubbed his belly. "Every year he did that."

"And every year you fell for it," Grandma said.

"You never did realize that Rich didn't even have a camera?" my dad added.

They all laughed—as if Rich had lived just long enough to give them a few good yuks. They were still laughing when I stood up.

"May I be excused, please?" I said.

There was another uneasy silence.

"No pie?" Grandma said.

"No. I don't want pie." My voice was rising, and I let it. "Maybe you can just let Rich go and get on with your lives, but I can't." I was yelling now, so I shoved the chair against the table. "Have fun!" was my parting shot.

Nobody stopped me. Not even my dad. He didn't look at me as I escaped from the dining room.

BACK TO THE BEGINNING

I didn't come out of my room the rest of the evening. I waited until everyone had gone sightseeing the next day before I emerged. Every year the whole family came to Boston for Christmas, and every year they saw the same things, as if history was going to change from one year to the next.

But in my case, it really *was* changing. Everything

ahead was going to be different from what it should've been because Rich wasn't there for me now.

I had a piece of pumpkin pie for breakfast. It tasted like posterboard, but anything I'd have eaten would've been the same. It had been that way since they told me my uncle Rich had "lost his battle" with cancer.

I never really thought he was going to. Sure, he'd lost his hair from the chemo and was tired a lot. But we had so much to do. He was saving my life as he fought for his own. I just didn't think either of us would lose.

The phone rang at about 2 p.m., and the voice on the other end caught me off guard.

"Carl, my man."

"Who's this?" I said. But I recognized it. Dan Dillon.

"This is Dan, dude. It hasn't been that long, has it?"

"I guess not," I said.

"Long time no see, dude, but we have short memories. We'll forget you haven't partied with us for six months. We got one goin' at 8 tonight. Gary's place."

"Whatever."

"Just thought we'd let you know, dude. Don't be a stranger."

I let the phone thud onto the hook. I hadn't said no. Six months ago—four months ago—before Rich died, I'd have said, "No, Dan, I don't party anymore," and Rich and I would've celebrated. But without him, I didn't say no. I left it a very possible whatever.

I got up, put my plate in the dishwasher, took a shower, and turned up the football game full blast, but the same thought kept chasing through my head. Drinking tonight would help me forget things for a while. It would be easy to go right back where I'd started because I didn't have Rich to answer to, and nobody else could fill that hole.

## GRIEF IN THE GROCERY STORE

I was getting dressed at 7 p.m. when Aunt Karen tapped on my door. She was the first one to approach me since I'd blown up at the table the day before.

"I'm being sent to replenish the supply of whipped cream and rye bread," she said through my door. "Come with me?"

"I kind of have plans," I said.

"Out-of-town grocery stores are scary places. If you don't come, I may get lost forever in the produce department."

I grumbled something, but knew Aunt Karen wasn't going to take no for an answer, so I followed her downstairs and plopped into the car.

When we were searching the dairy case I noticed Aunt Karen's eyes were red and puffy. She noticed that I noticed, and back in the car she drove slowly and inched up to the subject.

"I want to thank you," she said.

"For what?"

"For what you said at dinner yesterday. About us acting like Rich's death wasn't a tragedy."

"My dad's probably ticked at me because I ruined Christmas," I said.

"But you're right, it's a tragedy for me, too, and until yesterday I didn't really face that. Right away when Rich died, I told myself that he was with God now and there was no reason to grieve. But I forgot one important thing my little brother taught me. You have to take care of yourself, too, and that means dealing with your grief." I could hear the tears in her voice. "I've been putting off grieving, Carl, and that isn't healthy. Rich is okay now—but I'm not."

She reached over and patted my hand. "So thanks for reminding me."

"It's okay," I said.

It wasn't, really, for me—but Karen was on a roll. "I vote for a movie tonight. Point me in the direction of the nearest video store, and I'll rent."

## RUNNING SCARED

So I didn't make the party, but I dreamed about it that night. Dan had me pinned down on a leather chair and was pouring a Budweiser down my throat. I woke up kicking off the covers. I didn't want to be drinking in the dream, and I didn't want to do it for real. Rich had helped me to see that I had control over my decisions, that I could be tolerant of all kinds of people without getting hooked up with the wrong ones.

But Rich was gone, and not only had he taken his cackley laugh, great tennis arm, and his I-always-have-time-for-you attitude—he'd taken my courage.

I was ramming around the house early Saturday, trying to shake off the cobwebs of the dream, when Gramps came downstairs. It was time for his Christmas ritual.

"So you got up early to give me a hand with a shovel, eh, Carl?" he said.

"Sure, Gramps," I said. There was no use avoiding the confrontation that was sure to come over my outburst at the table. My parents would get their chance soon enough when everybody left tomorrow.

Gramps was methodical about shoveling snow, so he didn't say anything for a while. Halfway down the walk he looked at me sideways and said, "I chopped wood for three solid days after the funeral. Screamed at God the whole time."

I looked at him sharply.

"Told Him a thing or two—like He had no right to take my son away before he'd even had a chance to live—like He should've taken me because I already had my family and Rich didn't. I spoke my mind and swung that ax until I nearly did myself in." Gramps chuckled, an older version of Rich's contagious laugh. "God just sat up there and listened to me as He does. And then eventually I stopped screaming, and He started healing me. The thing is, He couldn't have started the cure if I hadn't let Him. Funny how that works."

I heard what he was saying—but he didn't understand. Grief wasn't making me scream anymore. It was fear. Without Rich, I was scared.

They called again Saturday, Dan and the rest. I told them they had the wrong number, and after Dan said, "Sure, dude. Eight o'clock tonight," I hung up. But I still didn't say, "No thanks, I don't drink."

The family sort of soft-stepped around me in the driveway the next morning with the good-byes. As soon as Uncle Bryan's car turned out of our street, I was headed for my room, but my dad put his hand on my shoulder—here it came.

"Your mother says it's time to take the lights down from the house," he said. "Give me a hand in the attic, would you?"

## THE HOLE IS FILLED

We'd found most of the boxes that we needed, and Dad still hadn't started yelling. He kept quiet as he rifled through a bunch of stuff in the corner. I grabbed a carton.

"Here's the box for the lights, Dad," I said.

"Well, would you look at this!"

Dad held a photo album and waved me over. Reluctantly, I joined him. He reverently turned the pages with me looking over his shoulder until his finger sprang to one picture.

"Now *there's* an oldie," he said.

I peered closely. "That isn't me, is it?"

"That's your uncle Rich. You look so much like him, it's uncanny."

"Who's that with him?"

My dad softly laughed the family laugh. "That's your old man. We were a team back then, Rich and me."

He let go of the album as I pulled it from him and stared hard at the photo. Dad, with a full head of hair and a face without worries, had an arm carelessly thrown around Uncle Rich's neck. Both of them looked like they were crazy about the world, crazy about each other.

"He was so much younger than me, but he was my little buddy," Dad said. "Followed me everywhere from the time he could walk—just like you did with him fifteen years later. It scared me when he got to be a teenager, though."

"Why?"

"He had a wild streak in him. He was a good young Christian—but he was so open, you know, curious. He wanted to know everybody and try everything. He could've gotten into a heap of trouble."

For the first time, I took my eyes from the picture. There was a sickening ache of familiarity in my stomach.

"Why didn't he?"

"The two of us worked it through. For some reason he always came to me instead of your grandparents—maybe because I was closer to his age. Of course, if anything had happened to me, he'd have found someone else to help him."

I looked down at the album. "You know about me, huh?"

"Yep."

My stomach wrenched. "How? Did Rich tell you?"

My father chuckled. "I'm not blind, Carl. I saw the signs when you were thirteen. But you had Rich, just like he had me. I knew you'd be okay."

The tears were close. I could hear them. We both sat in the silence and let them subside.

"What about now, Carl?" Dad said finally. "With Rich gone, I thought you were okay until this weekend. I knew you were depressed—that's normal. But you're afraid, aren't you?"

I could only nod.

"I helped one boy through the tough years, Son. I think I still have it in me to help another."

I fingered the edge of the photo album until the paper flaked in my hand. Dad squeezed my shoulder.

"Rich knew all the right things to say, because God was there coaching him. Rich may be gone, but God hasn't abandoned you. He uses what's here, and so should you."

I looked down again at the picture of the two young guys. For a minute, it was Rich and me laughing at the world. Man—I wanted to feel that way again.

Slowly, I closed the album and looked at my dad.

"You know those phone calls I've been getting?" I said.

He sat down, and I sensed a spirit had suddenly filled the attic. Maybe it was Rich. More than likely, though, it was God, filling up that hole in my life.

*Nancy N. Rue*

Nancy Rue, of Lebanon, Tennessee, novelist and short story writer, is a frequent contributor to contemporary and inspirational magazines. She is also the author of the Christian Heritage historical fiction series published by Focus on the Family.

HEADQUARTERS
OF · SANTA · CLAUS

# THE MIRACLE OF CHRISTMAS

---

*Justin Anderson's parents had showered him with money rather than love. Two years ago, he had lost his best friend to an irresponsible driver. Now it was Christmas, and he felt that nothing was right with his world.*

*And then . . .*

The brownstone dormitory across the street was a dark shadow against the graying sky, except for two squares of light that marked the superintendent's office on the ground floor. From the front room of his apartment in Westminster Court, Justin Anderson regarded the lights resentfully.

He sat forward in a garnet leather armchair, his handsome, rather arrogant face expressive of a vast discontent. He had been sitting there since five o'clock and now it was six-thirty, for he had nowhere to go except downtown to the ornate dining room of the Winfield Scott Hotel. It was Christmas Eve, he reflected moodily, and he had not a single friend to turn to in this one night of all the year when the spirit of good will and fellowship was paramount.

He could see, beyond the dormitory, the lights at the entrances to other buildings on the campus. They had never held any special significance for him, in spite of the alma mater song about "friendly lamps like starlight gleaming." He had long since decided that such sentiments were childish; college-boy stuff which he had always despised. The college meant nothing whatever to him, he reflected. As a matter of fact, nothing mattered except the deep, unending ache of loneliness that had become a constant part of him ever since Merton Hallock had walked smilingly out of their room over in the "old dorm," and had not come back.

Merton had been struck by an automobile driven recklessly by another undergraduate down University Drive. His ensuing death had left Justin Anderson with a great bitterness in his heart against his fellow students. Although it was midseason and he was admittedly the star of the team, he had resigned from the football squad; had given up his room in the dormitory and moved to an apartment across the street. At times, the realization that his friend would never return, that no resumption of the ideal relationship that existed between them could ever happen, would fill him with such seething anger that his massive body shook as if with a terrible fever. Mostly, though, his sorrow was just a dull ache that took from him all ambition, desire, and friendliness.

He became a recluse, living alone in his spacious apartment, with only Mrs. Connolly to share his self-imposed exile. He knew that his former friends considered him odd, gripped as he was by an obsession that he made no effort to throw off. He knew that they resented his abandonment of the football team of which he would have been captain in his senior year. He did not care. Instead, he lived in an inner world, haunted by Merton Hallock's smile—a smile he'd never see again.

Now, at six-thirty o'clock on Christmas Eve, he sat facing the square of darkness that was the dormitory and remembered the Christmas of his sophomore year. He had spent it with the Hallock family in a white New England house on the top of a high hill, with snow clinging to the branches of pine trees and the river a blue mirror of ice. That Christmas represented the greatest happiness he had ever known.

He wondered, as he heard Mrs. Connolly's step in the hallway, if he would ever find peace again. He did not think so. He was young, to be sure, only twenty-two; and yet, something had happened to him. The realization that he was not as other men worried him.

and yet he could think of nothing he could do about it. Long since, he had surrendered to his obsession. His lack of companions bothered him not at all, for he had no desire for friendship.

He became aware of Mrs. Connolly's presence in the room, and he turned without interest.

"Good evening!" she said, and switched on a floor lamp beside the piano.

Justin Anderson looked at her inquiringly. She had long since finished her duties for the day, and he had told her early in the evening that it would not be necessary for her to prepare his supper.

"I thought you'd be home," he said inadequately.

She seated herself at one end of the divan and fixed her eyes upon an intricate design on the Oriental rug at her feet.

"My son is going to be married the first of the week," she announced tonelessly. "I knew it was coming but thought that he would wait awhile."

Justin nodded.

"He'll be living with you, I suppose."

"No. He—he seems to want a place of his own. He can afford it, he says, and he wants to move to a better neighborhood. He asked me to go along, but I'm not needed now."

Justin was only vaguely aware of the unhappiness in her voice. "That's too bad," he said, and was seized, suddenly, by an impulse of generosity. "But you can keep on where you are. I'll see that you have enough for expenses, and a little more."

Mrs. Connolly shook her head. "I'm not talking

charity," she answered evenly. Suddenly her shoulders sagged. "It's being needed I'm wanting."

"It will come out all right." Justin stood up with a touch of embarrassment. "I'm going downtown now. Can I drive you home?"

"I'll stay here for a while if you don't mind, sir."

He drew on a fur coat, picked up his hat from the center table, and went downstairs. A gleaming coupe stood at the curb, and he slipped into the driver's seat. A man carrying bundles passed on the sidewalk and looked up enviously.

Justin drove through the center of town to the shining facade of the Winfield Scott. An obsequious doorman helped him to alight and gasped a grateful "Thank you, sir," as he realized the size of the tip that Justin gave him.

The hotel lounge was bright with color; holly wreaths hung from the chandeliers, and mistletoe was in inconspicuous places. In the dining room the orchestra was playing Christmas music. Justin tossed his coat to an attendant and entered.

He glanced without interest at the guests at adjoining tables: a young man and a starry-eyed girl absorbed in conversation; a family of four, dominated by a curly-haired boy who had spilled gravy on his bib. In the far corner, a man sat alone looking drearily out of a window.

Justin ordered a simple meal. Two boys came in, laughing. He recognized them as freshmen who lived in town. Approaching his table, they hesitated, as if they would have liked to join him, but at his curt nod they passed on. The orchestra played "Jingle Bells," and

Justin remembered again the Christmas he had spent with Merton Hallock in the New England hills.

Merton was gone now, and Christmas would never mean anything except tragic memories. Justin toyed with his food, a deep sense of unhappiness possessing him. Curiously, he found himself remembering other holiday seasons, half-forgotten years of his boyhood when selfish, too-rich parents had shunted him off to the care of hired tutors; of schools that permitted unwanted boys to remain during vacation for adequate compensation.

His parents were gone now, leaving him no inheritance but money; more than he needed, more than was good for him. He would gladly have traded it all for the memory of one kindly word.

The orchestra, concluding "Jingle Bells," laid down their instruments and shifted to an anteroom. The head waiter turned on the radio, and a mellow voice broke into reflections: "And on earth peace, good will toward men."

The voice trailed off into silence, and a moment later a jaunty announcer advised a waiting public that the "happy hour" was about to begin. Justin tossed a bill upon the table and went out to the lobby. He could see through the revolving door that it had begun to snow.

He loitered indecisively, dreading the return to his apartment but having nothing else to do. Gaily lighted windows along Main Street held no allure, and after a time he seated himself near the doorway. Men came into the hotel, knocking the snow from their hats; glanced at him curiously; and passed on. He found himself thinking about Mrs. Connolly. Obviously, she was unhappy over her son's approaching marriage. She had said something about not being needed anymore. That was a tragedy of maturing years, Justin reflected. An infinitely greater tragedy was to be young, without friends, without interests, with only a dull heartache that went on endlessly.

The dean of the college had talked to him about it; had told him in a memorable interview that other people had sustained losses and had carried on without bitterness, without discouragement. These other people, Justin had reminded the dean, had not been starved for affection through the long years of youth. The dean, not understanding, had called him a quitter, had said that he was morbid, and had dismissed him.

A shabbily dressed woman came into the lobby, followed by a little girl carrying a large bundle.

"I want to go home now and wait for Santa Claus," the child announced audibly.

Unexpectedly, Justin winced. He could not remember ever having believed in Santa Claus. Apparently some faith was still in the world, especially among children. After all, they had a right to that on Christmas Eve.

Not knowing exactly why he did so, Justin buttoned his raccoon coat and left the hotel. His car was parked near the entrance but, ignoring it, he sauntered down Main Street. It was not yet nine o'clock, and the store windows were lighted brilliantly. Men and women brushed past him, their heads bent to the storm. He heard smatterings of conversation: about lights for Christmas trees, the number of guests at dinner, a church service in the morning.

The snow fell steadily, beating against his upturned

face. On the corner of Bayard Street, while he waited for a moment, he heard the voices of a church choir. He was tempted to enter the big building from which the sounds emerged, but decided against it. Instead, he walked on for another hundred feet and sought relief from the storm by stepping into the entrance of a store. He recognized it as the Bon Ton, the largest department store in town, and he followed a stream of people inside. For some unaccountable reason, his feeling of depression had disappeared and with it went some of his self-pity and bitterness.

Without knowing just why he did so, he took the elevator to the toy department and wandered from counter to counter, wondering if it was too late to buy a few trinkets for youngsters like the curly-haired boy he had seen in the dining room of the hotel. He came finally to an alcove in which sat a rather bedraggled Santa Claus. Free for the moment, the man looked up and smiled wearily.

"I'm tired," he said, "and after tonight I lose my job."

Only a few children were in the department and they, apparently, had already made their needs known. Justin was about to pass on when he glimpsed a small boy with red hair coming out of the elevator. The boy had apparently been running, for his freckled face was flushed and he was breathing heavily. He hurried anxiously toward the alcove and, ignoring Justin, addressed the bewhiskered man in quavering tones: "Are you Santa Claus?"

Justin waited curiously. The youngster, he decided, was no more than six or seven years old. Curly hair the color of carrots made a crown for his face, which was covered with big, attractive freckles. His small nose was turned up saucily but his eyes, of clearest blue, regarded the man before him with intense earnestness.

"Are you Santa Claus?" he asked again.

"I guess I am, Son," the man answered.

"Are you sure you are?"

"I'm Santa, all right." The man glanced at Justin and grinned. "And what can I do for you?"

"You can give me something for Christmas."

"Santa Claus always gives things to little boys. What is your name, Son?"

"Jimmy."

The tired man's voice was surprisingly gentle.

"What would you like for Christmas, Jimmy?"

"I want a mother," the boy said.

A lump formed suddenly in Justin Anderson's throat. For the first time in many months, he forgot to think about himself.

"A *mother*?" Santa Claus repeated dazedly.

"Yes sir!" The red-headed boy spoke hurriedly. "I ain't never had one, only the matron over at the Children's Home. So I sneaked out tonight to find you, and—and I want one very bad, sir."

"Well, now—" The man who was paid to be Santa Claus looked up helplessly. "I don't know whether we have any mothers left or not," he said doubtfully.

"I want one very bad," pleaded the boy. He turned and looked directly into Justin's face, as if asking him to help.

"Jimmy," asked Justin Anderson, and was surprised at the gentleness of his voice, "Jimmy, boy, would—would a father do?"

The youngster regarded him judicially, and after a long moment, he spoke: "Yes, a father would do if—if he's a big man like you."

A mist of tears formed suddenly over Justin's eyes, and two big drops rolled down his cheeks. Justin had not been able to cry since Merton Hallock had left him that late afternoon in the old dormitory. Now he was crying openly and unashamed.

"Jimmy, if you're willing to come with me, I—I'll be your father," he said.

Santa Claus was looking at him over the boy's curly head.

"I can tell by your eyes that you mean it," Santa said. "You can adopt this youngster if he lives in the Children's Home. Have you got enough money?"

"Yes," answered Justin. He opened his wallet and drew out a bill of large denomination. "My name is Justin Anderson and I live in Westminster Court. Come up tomorrow, Santa, and have dinner with us."

Santa Claus's whiskers were slightly awry, but Jimmy didn't notice: "We ought to be gettin' home," he suggested.

"Take it easy, old man!" Justin reached forward and stuffed the bill in the pocket of Santa's robe. "We'll be seeing you tomorrow, Santa Claus."

"You're crying," Jimmy said.

Into his own big hand crept the hand of the freckled-faced boy. They stood for a moment facing Santa Claus, and for the first time in more than a year Justin saw his future clearly outlined. Mrs. Connolly would be needed now to help bring up Jimmy. He would have no more nights of bitterness, no aching void in his heart.

"Say," Jimmy protested, "ain't we ever going?"

"Yes," Justin told him gently, "we're going home. But first, we've got to buy some toys for Christmas and go around to the Home to make the proper arrangements, haven't we?"

"No," the boy answered. "I don't want nothing—but you. Can you fix it up at the Home?"

"Of course," Justin told him. He made the boy wait just a minute while he had a brief conference with Santa Claus. He lifted the red-headed boy in his strong arms and carried him through the snow to the gleaming coupe.

"This is swell," Jimmy said. "Santa Claus can do a lot of things, can't he?"

"Yes," Justin answered. "But I didn't know until tonight that he could perform miracles." He started the engine, and as the big car glided noiselessly past the church on the corner, he heard the sound of voices singing Christmas carols.

## Earl Reed Silvers

(1891–1948)

In addition to being an English professor at Rutgers University, director of Rutgers University Press, and editor of the Rutgers *Alumni Monthly*, Earl Reed Rivers was a prolific writer of stories and books for young people, especially boys and young men.

*Lanita Kampton*

# THE GIFT THAT NEVER WAS

*A frequently asked question is this: "Is this story true?" This never-before-published story you are about to read is true. It is also deeply disturbing, for it reveals cruelty almost beyond my comprehension—cruelty that could not but leave lifelong scars on the little girl. Yet, in spite of it all . . . well, you'll have to read the story.*

Six-year-old Sharon Carter was overjoyed when her mother asked her to go Christmas shopping with her. Sharon had never been allowed to linger in a toy department before. How her blue eyes sparkled as she saw bright-colored balls, trains, airplanes, and dolls of all sizes. Even colorful marbles caught her eyes.

"Mother, are we going to get a store-bought present for Christmas this year?" she questioned.

"I told you I'm not shopping for you kids. We don't have the money."

"Why are you buying presents then?"

"We're going to Aunt Bertha's for Christmas. It's only right we take something for her children."

Sharon couldn't remember her parents ever giving her a toy for Christmas or any other time. She sighed wistfully as she remembered the Christmas spent at her maternal grandparents'. She had been surrounded by toys. Then she remembered the heartbreak of being forced to place all the toys in a box to be sent to the mission field when she arrived home with her treasures.

Her sisters were given toys on their birthdays, but Sharon's birthday was right after Christmas. Mrs. Carter would remember Sharon's birthday on New Year's Day, but decided there had been enough goodies for a while, so a birthday cake was out of the question. Sharon couldn't be given a toy or her sisters would think it was for Christmas and want one too. For five years nobody told Sharon when her birthday was.

Sharon was frequently reminded that she had almost been given up for adoption at birth because she was not a boy. That, coupled with never having a birthday, made her feel she didn't belong in the family.

"Mother, could I hold that doll for just a minute?"

"No! You'll only feel bad when you have to put it back. Besides, you are too big for dolls now that you have a little brother."

Sharon had a doll but kept it well out of sight. She had to be very lonely before she would drag it out to play. The doll had been well used and discarded by her sisters before it was given to her. One arm was missing and a leg had been broken off just below the knee. The remaining toes and fingers were stubs. Sharon might have been able to play with it even then if the eyes had been different.

The doll reminded her of going to the city with her maternal grandmother. On a street of that city, a car had hit a pedestrian. Sharon was never able to forget how he looked. The doll reminded her of that accident victim. It had no eyelashes and only the white of its eyes showed. On the few occasions Sharon played with the hand-me-down doll, she would play nurse, bandaging the legs and the head around the eyes.

Sharon longed for a beautiful doll with shiny blonde hair like her own. She wanted it to say "Mama" when she picked it up. She could do without the ones that wet their diapers, though. Her brother did enough of that.

Sharon began to get excited about going to Aunt Bertha's for Christmas. She loved playing with her cousins, and the whole Carter family planned to be there. Her smile began to fade, however, as she remembered the last time the Carter family got together.

"What's the frown for?" her mother questioned.

"I was just thinking about the picnic at Rock Creek the last time we visited Grandma Carter."

"That should make you smile, not frown."

"I was feeling bad for Jack because everyone scolded him for something Beth did. I told Grandma Carter it was Beth that put her dish of food in the garbage so she could have cake, but Grandma said I was lying because Beth wouldn't let me play with her ball. It just makes me mad that everyone gets in trouble when it's Beth's fault."

"You had better change your attitude, young lady."

"But, Mom, I saw Beth do it. She looked all around to see if anybody was watching."

"Sharon!"

"It just couldn't be Jack. Uncle Jake said he had a hollow leg to fill."

"Sharon! I said that's enough."

For two days Sharon helped her mother bake, but at last the baking was done and the car was packed. Sharon and her two older sisters were dressed in their new look-alike dresses that their mother had made. The dresses didn't fit very well because Mrs. Carter did not have a pattern: she had just cut and sewed. Sharon's dress was uncomfortably tight in the sleeves and short in the waist.

"Mother, did we put the presents in the car that you bought when we went shopping?" Sharon asked.

"What presents?" thundered Mr. Carter.

Mrs. Carter came to Sharon's rescue, but not before the stitches in the sleeve of Sharon's new dress had been torn loose by her father's tight grip.

"I told you I bought a small gift for each of Bertha's

children. It would be rude not to since we are going to her house. I also had to buy an extra present for another child. Each child will get one," Mrs. Carter explained.

It was enough to set Sharon's heart pounding for joy. There would be a toy for Christmas this year! She went over in her mind the size and shape of all the toys she had helped her mother select. She hoped she would get one of them.

Everyone was given something to carry into Aunt Bertha's house. Then Sharon's sisters, Betty and Martha, were invited to Beth's room to see all the gifts she had already been given. Sharon followed quietly. Beth was showing Betty and Martha her glass tea set, which was on a beautiful bird's-eye maple table. Four child-sized chairs were positioned around it. The table was much nicer than the one Sharon admired while shopping with her mother.

On Beth's bed lay the biggest doll Sharon had ever seen. She was not able to resist the temptation of picking the doll up. It was almost as tall as she was, Sharon noted as she slid the doll's feet to the floor. She was so startled when it took a step that she let it topple.

"That was a present from Grandmother, and you were not to touch it!" Beth shouted angrily as she pushed Sharon roughly to the door.

"I didn't invite you to my room, so don't come back," were Beth's parting words.

"Are you making trouble again?" Grandma Carter questioned. "Here, you've torn your new dress already. Shame on you!"

Sharon bit her lip to keep from saying that her father had torn her new dress when he grabbed her.

"Sharon, come and play with Andy," called her mother. "He doesn't like the playpen, but the floor is too cold for him to crawl around on. Someone might trip over him here in the kitchen, and I must help with dinner."

It wasn't long before more cousins arrived and were ushered into Beth's room. Sharon could hear the shouts of laughter behind that door. Everyone (except Sharon) was having a good time. After looking forward so long to playing with the cousins, it was disappointing to have to babysit.

"If you would just go to sleep, I could go back to Beth's room and join the tea party. It's all your fault, you know," Sharon muttered while rocking and patting Andy's back.

Sharon was given a plate of food to feed Andy. The whipped potatoes and baked winter squash went okay, but he spat the mashed green beans all over her and the kitchen wall.

"Good thing green is my favorite color or I'd object to you putting it all over my face," Sharon chuckled as she wiped her face with a paper towel. She didn't get angry with Andy, for he was the only friend she had.

After dinner everyone gathered in the living room to sing Christmas carols. Sharon loved singing, especially "Joy to the World," which she sang with all her might. Her father frowned at her, so she just pretended she was singing on the rest of the songs. She didn't want the Christmas toy to be taken away from her before she got it.

Soon it was time to open the gifts. In the middle of the room were two washtubs: one for boys' presents and one with gifts suitable for girls. Each child was to take a turn choosing a gift out of the appropriate tub. There were other brightly wrapped packages piled here and there around the room.

Several packages were taken to Sharon's mother to open for Andy first, because it was time for him to go to bed. Aunt Bertha had knit him a beautiful red sweater with a matching cap. Sharon recognized the pull toy as one she had helped her mother purchase. She glanced at her mother, who immediately put her index finger up to her lips and glanced apprehensively at her husband. Sharon knew she must not question why Andy was getting a store-bought toy from her mother.

There was also a boy doll dressed in overalls. Everyone laughed when Andy tried to kiss it.

One by one each child's name was called, and each chose a package. There was one box in the girls' tub with pretty pink tinfoil wrapping and a big silver bow. Sharon had never seen anything so beautiful. She held her breath as Beth's name was called. If it was there after Beth picked her package, Sharon was sure to have it. Beth picked up the beautiful pink box, and Sharon was crestfallen.

*Oh, well, I'm going to have a toy of some kind*, she consoled herself.

She couldn't believe what happened next. Aunt Bertha lifted the pink package from Beth's arms, and Beth was encouraged to select another present.

Sharon's name was called. She walked over and picked up the pink-and-silver package. She set it aside, however, for in the bottom of the tub was a package the exact shape and size of the doll she had wanted to hold in the store.

"You have to take the first box you picked up," Aunt Bertha admonished.

The pink box was Sharon's after all.

Sharon noted George's toolbox filled with tools and Martha's silver brush, comb, and mirror set. Betty had a storybook doll with a real storybook accompanying it. By now, Beth had her present unwrapped. It was a doll with its own pj's.

Slowly, Sharon unwrapped the pretty pink box, savoring every moment of anticipation.

"You be careful with that wrapper, I'd like to have it to make a winter bouquet. That tinfoil is just the thing to cover oats," Grandma Carter called from across the room.

Sharon remembered brightly colored oat bouquets shimmering in the slightest breeze and gladly passed Grandma Carter the pink tinfoil.

"I'll take that nice bow. You'll just crush it," piped in Aunt Lanora. Sharon passed it to her.

After removing an enormous amount of newspaper, Sharon found a matchbox in the bottom. Eagerly she opened it and found—a single penny. Everyone laughed and jeered at her disappointment.

"If you hadn't been so greedy and wanted the biggest and best, you'd have gotten a toy like everyone else," scolded Uncle Jake.

"Sharon, bring me that penny. If you leave it where Andy could get it, he might put it in his mouth and choke," declared her mother.

Sharon dutifully handed over the penny and dashed

from the room. Jeers of "That'll teach you" and "Spoiled sport" drifted after her. Sharon determined to run out of the house and hide in the row of huge poplar trees along the road, but Andy started whimpering as she passed.

"Hey, Stinker, be a good boy and don't make a fuss," Sharon whispered as silent tears trickled down her cheeks. "Everyone in the other room is having a good time and won't want to hear you." But Andy cried on, refusing to be ignored.

"You win! I'll change you and fix a bottle. Then you can go back to sleep.

"I wish you'd hurry and grow up so you could play with me," Sharon added.

She started humming "Silent Night" as she sat in the middle of the cold utility-room floor rocking Andy. She began to think about the first Christmas and how baby Jesus was born in a barn. *His folks must have been poor if a barn was the only place they could afford to stay,* she reasoned.

*I don't suppose Jesus had many toys when He was growing up,* she concluded.

Suddenly she felt as if she were holding baby Jesus in her arms instead of Andy. A light shone upon his face. A delicious warmth spread through Sharon as he looked up at her and chuckled, then encircled her neck with his chubby little arms. Indescribable joy filled her heart. She was loved. A doll could never return her love as this babe in her arms did.

Uncle Ron was amazed at seeing Sharon holding her brother with a serene smile on her face. He had not heard the back door open, so he knew she had stayed inside. But he expected to find her in the corner in tears.

The realization that someone had entered the room brought Sharon out of her daydream. She looked up at Uncle Ron with a smile that made her eyes sparkle. He remembered Beth having a beautiful smile like Sharon's when she was younger, but now her face pouted most of the time. Uncle Ron smiled at Sharon as he lifted the sleeping baby from her arms and tucked him into the travel bed. He then picked Sharon up and set her on the freezer chest. Reaching down into his pocket he drew out a silver dollar. Sharon shook her head and refused to take it from him.

"I already got my gift."

Without saying a word, Uncle Ron reached for Sharon's left foot and removed the shoe. After placing the silver dollar in the toe of the shoe, he returned it to her foot. He then lowered her to the floor.

"I want you to remember something, dear. The girl worthwhile is the girl who'll smile when everything goes plumb wrong."

Uncle Ron never said more than a word or two at a time, so without saying more he slipped out the back door.

Sharon carried the image of holding baby Jesus and Uncle Ron's thoughtfulness close to her heart as she entered the living room.

"Did you have a good cry?" Martha jeered.

"You look like the cat that ate the canary," Aunt Bertha snipped.

Sharon wiggled her toe against the silver dollar and smiled, then sat down to watch Grandpa Carter open his gift. She knew she had been given a gift more precious than all the gifts on Grandma Carter's lap or at cousin Beth's fingertips. Sharon had held baby Jesus—and He loved her.

*Lanita Kampton*

Lanita Kampton lived and wrote in Madras, Oregon, the second half of the twentieth century.

# A BOY NAMED JOHN

*Once upon a time, the greatest Christmas gift of all was an orange. A simple orange such as we throw away when we fail to eat it at its peak of ripeness.*

*What would it have been like to long for such a gift all year long—then, at the last minute, to lose it?*

*That's what happened to John.*

❄ ❄ ❄

*A number of people have written us, saying that they've been looking for this story for years. We've found it at last!*

In the early 1800s, a fourteen-year-old boy named John lived in an English orphanage along with several other children. At that time orphanages were dreaded, and only very underprivileged children who had no family and no one to care for them were placed there. To be an orphan meant being both unwanted and unloved.

The orphanage where John lived was a cold, damp, old brick building. John shared a bed on the floor with other children. Aside from that meager corner of existence, John had nothing to call his own. Nothing to ensure self-esteem. Nothing to ensure self-respect. The orphanage was administered by a master and his wife who were themselves the results of meager backgrounds. They were short on love and high on discipline. No childlike play. No expressions of compassion. No understanding. No love.

At the orphanage, every day of the year was spent working. The children worked in gardens. They cleaned, sewed, and cooked for wealthy families. They scrubbed the steep, cold stairs of the orphanage. They were up at dawn and usually received only one meal a day.

John had absolutely *nothing* to call his own. Nothing that was his, and only his. None of the children did. Oh, occasionally an old rag could be salvaged and John would tie a knot in the end to simulate the head of a doll for some small girl, or maybe a perfectly round pebble could be stuck in a small boy's hand to play marbles with, when the master wasn't looking. The master, however, was always looking—nothing escaped him.

On only one day of the year the children did not work. John had been in the orphanage long enough to look forward with delight and anticipation to this special day. Christmas. On that day each child received a gift, the one time of the year when all received something to call their own. That special gift was an orange.

Now, to us who live in America and have an abundance of citrus trees, this would not necessarily be special, but in old England, and to John and his orphan companions, it was a rare and special treat. It had an unusual aroma of something they smelled only at Christmas. The children prized their oranges so much that they often kept them for days, weeks, even months—protecting them, smelling them, touching them, and loving them. Sometimes they tried to savor and preserve them for so long that the oranges would rot before the children ever peeled them to enjoy the sweet juice inside. The children would say, "I will keep mine the longest this year." All year long they talked about the coming Christmas. They all determined that this year they would keep their oranges a long, long time.

John always took great care of his orange, holding it tenderly and carefully so as not to bruise it. He usually slept with it. He would put it right by his nose to smell its goodness. He would dream of children all over the world, smelling the sweet aroma of oranges. It gave him security and a sense of well-being. His dreams were filled with good food and a life different from this meager existence.

❄ ❄ ❄

One particular year, John was overjoyed by the Christmas season. He was becoming a man. He was feeling changes in his body and knew he was becoming stronger. Soon he would be old enough to leave the orphanage. Thus he was unusually excited about Christmas. This year he was determined to save his orange, knowing that if he preserved it very carefully, kept it cool, and did not drop it, he would be able to eat it on his birthday in April.

Christmas Day finally came. The children were so excited. As he entered the big dining hall, John could smell cooked meat, a luxury he had enjoyed only a few times in his lifetime. In his excitement and because of his oversized feet, John tripped, causing a disturbance. Immediately the master roared, "John, leave the hall—and there will be no orange for you!" John's heart broke. He began to cry. So the small children wouldn't see his anguish, he turned and ran swiftly back to his cold room and corner. What was there to look forward to now? He could almost taste the food he had smelled. He was happy for the other children, but brokenhearted for himself. The minutes went by very, very slowly. How could he possibly ever make it through another year at this orphanage?

Then, he heard the door open and a number of the children enter. Little Elizabeth, with her hair falling over her shoulders, a smile on her face, and tears in her eyes, held out a piece of rag to John. "Here, John," she said. "This is for you."

John, being remembered by her, reached for the bulge in her hand. As he lifted back the edges of the rag, he saw a big, juicy orange, all peeled and quartered. Then he realized what they had done. They had peeled their oranges and by each giving a section of their orange, they had created a big, beautiful orange for him.

❄ ❄ ❄

John never forgot the love his friends had shown him that Christmas. After he grew to manhood John became very successful and wealthy. But he never forgot that orange sacrificially assembled for him so long ago. Every year he would send oranges all over the world to orphanages and to children everywhere. His desire was that no child would ever again celebrate Christmas without a special Christmas gift.

# THE CHRISTMAS GIFT

*Maggie MacLeod was having it out with the Lord. It just wasn't fair to be lying there bedridden, unable to cook, to clean the house, to shop for Christmas gifts. All she could do was lie there while the family buried her in presents.*

*It just wasn't fair!*

Maggie MacLeod, lying in the big four-poster bed upstairs, wrinkled her nose unhappily as she sniffed the unmistakable odors wafting up from her daughter's kitchen—mince pies fresh from the oven. She turned her white-crowned head on the pillow and stared gloomily out the window, her mood as somber as the gray December sky.

"A fine state I've come to, Lord," she muttered rebelliously. "Laid out stiff as a board the day before Christmas, when you know I should be in my own kitchen, making my own pies, stuffing my own turkey!" Living by herself for so many years before she'd had that stroke last August and had to be moved to Margaret's, she'd fallen into the habit of chatting quite informally with the Lord as she went about her work. "I feel so plagued useless!"

It had been bad enough to have Margaret waiting on her hand and foot all fall when goodness knows she had enough to do with her husband and the five-year-old twins. But now, to be bedded in on this festive day—with everybody whipping around getting ready for the coming of relatives and the big dinner—and worst of all—her work-gnarled hands clenched under the bedclothes as her glance fell on the pile of gaily wrapped packages on the table in the corner, waiting for her to open them—*no presents to give to anybody at all.*

No one but the Lord, with whom she had discussed the matter off and on for months, knew how this problem had galled her, right from the beginning. For it was just about the time she'd become helpless that she'd usually start working on Christmas presents. Knitted mittens, scarves and sweaters, yarn dolls, intricately crocheted doilies, hooked rugs—articles like these, not only for her family but for a host of friends and neighbors—had formerly kept her evenings busy and full of glowing thoughts from the end of summer right on up past Thanksgiving. Not to mention plans for her annual party for the eight Sargent children down the street, Yule decorations for the church, fruit cakes for the Old Ladies' Home, and what not!

But now! Not able to make things with her hands and not enough money to commission somebody to buy gifts, what with doctor bills and her absolute insistence on paying a bit for her board and care here (they'd had a battle almost to the death over that, with Margaret bawling, if she couldn't take care of her very own mother, and her husband, Bill, roaring he wasn't that bad off, to have to take money from a sweet, sick old lady, and so on)—well, even the Lord hadn't seemed to come up with an answer to this one.

Downstairs the clock struck one. Mrs. MacLeod sighed and turned her face to the pillow. *Go to sleep, you old fool,* she told herself. *Take your nap like a nice old granny or you'll be even crosser when the folks arrive this afternoon.*

*Tomorrow by this time all the presents will have been opened, no one will remember who gave who what, and the hoopla will be over for another year. They're all probably fed up with crocheted doilies anyway.* And having convinced herself of absolutely nothing, she wearily closed her eyes.

Two seconds later, however, the creaking of that third-from-the-top step of the stairway alerted her to the fact that someone was coming up. She had made it a point never to mention that creak for fear Bill would come bustling up with his handyman kit and do something about it. That noise gave her the warning she needed to compose herself when she'd been having a blow-off session between herself and the Lord.

"Oh, Mother, did I wake you?" her daughter said reproachfully. "I was just going to tell you that I'm running downtown on a couple of last-minute errands. I'm sure I'll be home before the gang arrives."

"Send the twins up here then," Maggie answered. "There's too much for five-year-olds to get into downstairs today." She smiled to herself thinking of odd-shaped packages under the tree, pies cooling on the back porch, bowls of nuts just waiting for the nutcracker.

"I'm taking them with me; this is your nap time," Margaret said firmly.

"You may be thirty-five years old, but you're still my child and I say they're staying," Mrs. MacLeod replied just as firmly, though her eyes twinkled. "Don't forget I've got twenty-four hours a day from which to choose my sleeping time."

"Oh, Mother, you're wonderfully impossible," Margaret laughed. "All right, they wanted to stay here, anyway. If they get too frisky, send them outside to play; their wraps and boots are all laid out in the hall. I should be home in an hour," she called back as she hurried out of the room.

❄ ❄ ❄

Two minutes later what sounded like a herd of elephants thundered up the steps and tow-headed Ronny and Mark burst in.

"We're s'posed to be quiet and peaceful 'cause this is rest hour," Mark chanted mischievously as he hurled himself into the rocking chair by the window.

"Look out, you'll go clean over backward like you did the other day," Maggie warned anxiously.

"Finish the story you started yesterday, Granny, the one about the elves at the North Pole," Ronny pleaded, seating himself at the foot of the bed.

Mark stopped rocking. "Yeah, please, Granny, what happened to the elf who wouldn't take his turn shoveling snow? Somethin' awful?" he asked hopefully.

"Well, now, what do you think should happen to him?" Granny asked. "Remember that Saturday morning when you boys refused to sweep the walks like you were supposed to?"

"H-m-m." Mark raised his eyebrows and looked at Ronny.

"But shoveling snow is different," Ronny protested. "That's fun!"

"Because it's more of a novelty to you," Granny said. "For the elves in that snowbound land it was just an old run-of-the-mill job."

Mark looked out the window. "I wish there was snow here now," he said, scowling at the brown grass and the bare black tree trunks outside.

Ronny joined his brother and his little brow furrowed, too. "Yes, Granny, it's just gotta snow!" he said. "We asked for sleds for Christmas, and the way Mom and Dad roll their eyes around when we talk about it—we think we're going to get them—and what if we can't use them tomorrow?" His voice rose to an anxious crescendo.

"And besides," Mark added, "it just doesn't look like Christmas this way."

"Well," Granny said weakly, "there wasn't any snow for the first Christmas; the baby Jesus was born in a warm country." Even as she spoke she knew that was scant comfort to a young one.

"But this is a cold country," Ronny insisted, coming back to the bed. "Granny, do you think it *might* snow?"

"Mercy on us, child, who knows?" Granny chuckled. Then she added seriously, "You'll just have to be brave about it. As your grandfather used to say on a still, cold morning, 'Maybe 'twill snow, and maybe 'twont. Either way, it's God's good world.'"

Bringing the thought down to a five-year-old level, she went on, "If it doesn't snow, the pond will be better for skating. I'll bet you could get your Uncle Rob to take you down after dinner tomorrow."

"Well . . ." Ronnie said uncertainly, looking a little less desperate.

"Hey," Mark shouted suddenly, "here's a car coming in the driveway. It's Uncle Rob and—everybody!"

"Land sakes, they're early," Maggie cried excitedly. "They must have left home at the crack of dawn. Quick, run down and let them in." But she spoke to an empty room: the boys were already halfway down the stairs.

For a moment the bitter mood of the noon hour assailed her again. To think that she couldn't rush to the door herself, wiping her pumpkin-sticky hands on her big white apron, throwing open her door and her heart to welcome her children home. Guiltily she brushed from her mind the fleeting thought that it might have been better if she'd just passed away that night last August.

❄ ❄ ❄

In a few short minutes the babbling in the downstairs hall began to sound closer and closer and then all at once the whole lot of them were there, crowding around the bed, stooping to kiss her cheek: her eldest daughter, Ellen, as chic as ever in spite of her forty-four years, with her equally smart-looking husband, Brad; her youngest child, Rob, and his wife, Sue, carrying the baby of the clan, little year-old Peggy.

Maggie eyed them all lovingly.

The twins appeared at the door staggering under a pile of gaily wrapped packages. "Guess what, Granny, they brought all these for you!" Mark shouted. "We'll put 'em under your own tree." He and Ronny deposited their load on the corner table where Margaret had placed a dainty little silver-dipped evergreen.

Maggie winced. Having nothing to give, it would have been far more comfortable to receive nothing.

Ellen caught the look. "You're tired, Mother," she said quickly. "We shouldn't all have piled in on you like this." With her sleekly cropped head, she motioned the others toward the door.

"I'm all right," Maggie protested, but the family began to edge out anyway, with much talk about having to feed the baby, unpack their bags, and so on.

"I guess I was selfish to reserve the first visit with you for myself," Ellen smiled.

"I'll see them all in due time; sit down, Ellen, you look tired," Maggie said abruptly. With a mother's perceptive eye she had seen a shadow behind the brave, beautiful make-up of her daughter's face.

"Oh, it's just the Christmas rush," Ellen began vaguely.

"Is it?" Maggie said levelly.

"Well, of course, you know it was a disappointment that Dick and his wife decided to spend the holidays with her family. After all, she had the crowd at her house for the wedding last summer."

Maggie was quiet for a sympathetic moment. Then she said, "How old is Dick, Ellen?"

Ellen stared. "Come now, Mother, don't tell me you've forgotten the age of your first grandchild. You know he's twenty-two."

"Wasn't that just about the age you were when you brought your new husband home to us for Christmas? Remember, he had a mother, too."

Ellen blushed. "I deserved that," she said humbly. "But I guess Dick's not coming was kind of a last straw." She hesitated.

Maggie waited.

"I shouldn't bother you with my little troubles, Mother." Ellen moved over and sat on the edge of the bed. "But somehow, in this quiet room, and you listening, just like you used to when I'd come home from a school date, and pour out all my dreams and troubles—"

"Go on, child," Maggie said gently.

"Well, it just seems I've been growing more and more restless the last few years. When Dick went away to school I threw myself into committee meetings and clubs and all that. But even those things don't satisfy me now, and Brad's so busy at the office—"

"Restlessness is a good thing," Maggie interrupted.

"It keeps you from being satisfied with yourself. All you've got to do is head it in the right direction."

"But you don't know what it's like, Mother," Ellen protested. "You seem so peaceful and content—"

"Content!" Maggie exploded. "I hate it here! I just hate it!" She pounded a fist on the quilt.

Ellen jumped. "Mother, for goodness sake!" She glanced toward the open door.

"Oh, I don't mean it that way," Maggie said hastily. "Margaret's family's been wonderful. I mean here—in bed, in this position"—she held a hand out horizontally. "What good am I doing anybody lying here like this?"

"What good?" Ellen echoed slowly.

"Of course, what else?" Maggie snapped. "I've had a full life, Ellen, and so, now, have you," she went on more gently. "You've gotten your man, raised your child, made your place in the community. A woman has to work and sometimes even fight for those things. She has to think of herself and her second self—her closest ones.

"But now you can afford to set your sights a little wider, kind of get out of yourself, and then there's the whole wonderful, maddening, messed-up world waiting for you to set it to rights!" Maggie ended enthusiastically.

"Well, Mother, that's quite a speech," Ellen laughed, but there was a breathless little catch in her voice.

"There, now, I got carried away with myself," Maggie said, chuckling. She reached down the bed and patted Ellen's hand. "But lying here alone, all kinds of crazy notions run through my old head."

Ellen sat up purposefully. "They aren't crazy notions,

Mother," she said firmly. "They're the ideas you've been living by, all those things you've been so busy at for years, in the neighborhood, at the church, with us—"

Her eyes took on a faraway look and she went on, half to herself. "Of course, things are different in a big city, but there's the Volunteer Bureau and the Red Cross unit that's been trying for years to get me to help. The minute I get back to town I'll—"

❄❄❄

A head appeared around the half-closed door. "I don't suppose a man has a chance with two gabbing women?" Rob grinned as he walked over to his mother's bedside.

"*One* gabbing woman," Ellen corrected laughingly. "Mother's really in good form today. Here, take my seat for the lecture; I'd better get down to the kitchen and start doing my part." She winked at Maggie and strode out of the room.

"Ellen getting a lecture?" Rob raised his eyebrows. "She seems to have things well under control."

"She has problems," Maggie said briefly.

"I don't know what." Rob looked puzzled. "She's got everything: money, position—if I were in her shoes I wouldn't complain."

"Robby, what's eating you?" Maggie's quick ear had caught a trace of bitterness in his tone.

"Oh, Mother, Christmas Eve isn't the time to be airing one's troubles. Besides, we were supposed to be coming here to cheer *you*!"

"Nonsense!" Maggie waved a hand impatiently. "Out with it, boy."

Rob looked down at his shoes. "I've been passed up for that job as head of the department at the factory."

"Oh," Maggie said quietly.

There was a moment's silence between them.

Then Rob burst out, "It isn't only that job, Mom, it's something more. It's hit me that I'm just not the executive type; I don't look forward to bringing a briefcase full of work home every night, lying awake stewing over the company's finances, playing golf on weekends with the right people. Here I am twenty-nine years old—what's to become of me?" He ran his hands wildly through his close-cropped red hair.

"Robby, dear," Maggie said slowly, "it seems to me there are two ways for a man to grow—up or outward. The one kind pushes himself up, up, at almost any cost, to be a success in a worldly way. The other kind, well, he kind of spreads himself. His time, his energies, flow out in little side channels—to his family, his friends, his hobbies, his community—like your father," she finished softly.

"Yes?" Rob was staring at her.

"Yes," Maggie repeated. "It probably seemed perfectly natural to you that your dad always had time to put you to bed, time to take care of the minister's flower garden because he had a knack for growing things, time to sponsor that campaign to save those beautiful elms along Main Street when the state wanted the road widened."

"He was always up to something, wasn't he?" Rob smiled reminiscently.

"If, however," Maggie continued, "he had lived and

breathed only for that grocery store of his, he might have wound up a supermarket tycoon."

Rob nodded thoughtfully.

"The world needs both kinds, Rob, and maybe you'll be like your father; and who's to say his kind doesn't do as much for the world as the strictly go-getter type?" Maggie's voice rang with conviction.

"You've sure given me something to think about," Rob said slowly.

"Then go somewhere and think about it," Maggie rejoined, "and let me catch my forty winks, or I'll be too tired to listen to the family carol-singing tonight."

When her son had kissed her lightly and gone out, Maggie turned her face toward the pillow and sighed, "Well, Lord, those babies of mine are still having troubles. Once it was bumped knees and broken dolls—I could do something about *that.* But now their need is greater than ever and what do I have to give? . . . Christmas time, and nothing to give—just between You and me, Lord, it *hurts.*" And then, because she really was exhausted, she drifted off to sleep.

❄ ❄ ❄

The next thing Maggie knew she was opening her eyes to the sound of footsteps and laughing voices outside her room somewhere. Struggling to consciousness she heard a child giggle—that would be Ronny—and then an untrained chorus caroling out "Deck the Halls with Boughs of Holly." The song came to her louder and louder, accompanied by the tramp of many feet on the stairs. Then a scuffling outside her door, and a high treble stage whisper, "Open it quick; I can't hold this stuff a minute longer!"

The door burst open, and Maggie's eyes were now really open wide as she saw the whole family troop in, each person with armfuls of gear. Rob was already beginning to unfold the legs of three card tables; Margaret was at his side with Christmas tablecloths and napkins and a basket of silverware. Mark was precariously balancing a tray of red and white nut cups; Ronny hugged a pair of silver candlesticks with tall, unlighted tapers. The rest, similarly laden, were still milling around the door, their singing punctuated with chuckles over Maggie's wildly amazed expression.

Then, to everyone's horror, her chin began to tremble and she turned her head quickly away.

"Granny, we've come up to have Christmas Eve dinner with you. Don't you want us to?" Ronny cried, running anxiously toward the bed.

"Oh, Mother, it's just too much for you!" Margaret, still hugging the tablecloths, came over to the other side of the bed. "But we thought it would be such fun to surprise you—"

Maggie's face came out of the pillow with a swift jerk. "Too much for me, nonsense," she blurted out. "It's just that it makes me feel all the worse."

"Worse?" Margaret looked alarmed.

"To think I've no presents for you—any of you—for the first time since any of you've been born—" Maggie's eyes traveled painfully to the pile of packages under the little tree on the table. "There now, it's out, what's been driving me daffy these long days since."

Margaret was the first to recover. "Mother," she said

fondly, "do you know how many neighbors envy me for having such a wonderful built-in babysitter, as they call you? When I think of all the times you've entertained the twins to keep them out from under my feet—"

"And the example in this house of patience and fortitude—" her quiet husband, Bill, put in unexpectedly.

"Alas, age has touched the poor woman's mind," Rob said solemnly. "Else why would she think a crocheted necktie a more valued gift than, well, a philosophy of life in a capsule?"

"What your children are trying to tell you, Mother, in their stumbling way," Ellen said, smiling, "is that you yourself are the finest gift of all: the life you've lived, the things you stand for, your just *being* here when we need help—" She broke off, and the others nodded in agreement.

"Well!" Maggie said quaveringly, after a moment of stunned silence, "who's making speeches now?"

Just then one of the twins who had been standing by the window suddenly cried out, "Hey, look, it's snowing!"

Everyone looked outside at the falling snow.

"The snow had begun in the gloaming," Rob chanted laughingly.

"Turn out the lights for a minute," Margaret said impulsively. "We can see it better."

Bill reached over and flicked the wall switch. Ellen, who had been about to light the candles, stayed her hand.

The twins pressed their noses against the lower part of the cold windowpane.

From the dusky recess of her bed corner Maggie looked out over the little ones' heads to the velvet blue-black curtain of evening, filigreed with falling flakes of white. Even after sixty-five seasons of this, she still caught her breath at its magic beauty.

There was a moment's deep silence in the room.

Then Bill switched the lights back on and Ronny turned from the window. "Well, Granny," he said jubilantly, "the snow really came. Now we won't have to be brave!"

"What is the child prattling about?" Ellen laughed.

"Oh, the twins and I were having a little talk this afternoon." Granny smiled mysteriously. She cleared her throat. "Well, folks, since you've got this wacky notion of eating Christmas Eve dinner in a bedroom—" she tried without success to look severe—"you'd better get those tables set. The food must surely be growing cold."

As the clatter and bustle of preparation began again she closed her eyes. "Thank you, Lord," she whispered gratefully, "thank you for *everything*."

*Dorothy Boys Kilian*

Dorothy Boys Kilian wrote for inspirational magazines in the mid-twentieth century.

# THERE'S A SONG IN THE AIR

---

*Amy Martin wanted nothing more to do with small children. Just the thought of them and what she and her husband had lost three years before hurt too much.*

*Then came that intrusive little face staring at her through the ivy. Came. And went.*

Amy Martin took the second-best broom from its corner on the back porch and went out to sweep the walk under the grape arbor.

The bricks here were uneven, and some of them were mossy and held the moisture. If ice collected Thomas might slip and fall when he took the trash out to the alley. At least that was the excuse she gave herself. But she really wanted to see if the child was there again this morning.

She didn't like to admit it to herself, but something about the whole affair gave her a slightly uncomfortable feeling. For three weeks, ever since she had first been aware of the face staring at her through the December tangle of vines on the back fence—the fence that shut her property off from the alley—she had not quite felt that she belonged to herself. Her privacy was crumbling, and all because a strange child insisted on watching her whenever she came out the back door.

It was a mysterious kind of thing. There was no young child whom she knew of in any of the homes whose back gates opened on the alley. And this child was a silent, shabby little thing, acting as though she knew she shouldn't be here. The one time when Amy had spoken to her and said, "Where's your home, little one?" the child had stared at her, then had run down the alley and disappeared. She had dropped one faded, dirty mitten in her flight. The mitten, washed and mended, now lay on the shelf on the back porch. Amy planned to give it to her this morning.

❄❄❄

The bricks of the wide old walk under the arbor were laid in herringbone style, and even in winter fine green lines of moss outlined the pattern. In a way the arbor was like Thomas and Amy Martin. It clung a little to the past, as though, if it waited, it might recapture what had gone.

In this respect, too, it was like the quiet, polished house that also seemed forever to be waiting; like the attic where the dollhouse stood in its dust cover of unbleached muslin; where the little beaver muff lay in the holly red box, swathed in tissue and mothballs; where the bright music box waited to play its tinkling tune of Christmas:

*There's a song in the air!*
*There's a star in the sky!*

Amy swept carefully, working her way to the very end of the arbor and the alley gate before she allowed herself to look. But there was no small face, framed in an old blue woolen scarf, peering through the palings. Amy was aware of a sharp sense of—something—in her breast, relief, no doubt.

"Well," she said half aloud, knocking the broom against the fence to clear it of leaves and twigs. "Maybe the visitation is over. Maybe every move I make won't be watched now." And just to be sure she was at last completely free of the black eyes she unlatched the back gate and looked searchingly up and down the alley.

It was empty, except for the neat row of trash cans set

out beside each householder's gate in readiness for the weekly collection. As she stood there, the Warrens' cat, pursued by the Adams' dog, streaked past her and up one post of the arbor. From the security of the top, her sharp, indignant hiss was loud in the silence of the alley. But there was no child. Amy latched the gate, then went slowly back up the walk to the house.

❄ ❄ ❄

"What kind of child is it?" Thomas asked her at supper. Of all the silly questions a husband could ask, this was about the silliest.

"What kind of child? Why, just a plain child. You know what a child is, Tom."

He ignored her heavily ironic tone. "How old, Amy? Girl or boy?"

"Girl—I'd say she's five or six years old. . . ." She watched him narrowly but there was no change in the expression on his face. "Mostly eyes. She just stands there and watches me with those big, black eyes. Never speaks."

"Wonder why she isn't in school in the daytime. But I can't see anything to get upset about, dear. Probably just thinks you're a funny old woman. And how right she is. . . ." He laughed and passed his plate for more peach pie. But the words and the laugh didn't sound gay and impertinent, as she knew he meant them to.

She tried to match his effort. "I don't mind being called funny, but *old*—Thomas Martin, if you begin calling me an old woman now, when I'm thirty-seven, what will you be calling me when I'm sixty? Anyway, you're two years older than I am, don't forget." But the words sounded hollow to her. And when she looked across the table into Tom's face, she saw the old wound there, the shadow that was somehow deeper at Christmas than at other times, or harder to mask, perhaps.

She put an extra spoonful of peaches on his plate and passed it back to him.

"Want to go to a movie? Dickens' *A Christmas Carol* is playing downtown somewhere. The lights might be pretty tonight, too."

"No, thank you, dear. I feel a little tired tonight. Let's just sit by our own fire."

"Suits me." He got up and went around the table and bent down, putting his lips against her cheek. She reached up and held his face against hers for just an instant.

"If we could just stop the clock—or better yet, set it up into the New Year."

"Amy—have you thought maybe we're alone too much these days? I mean—maybe we've—"

The doorbell chimed musically through the house, and there was a sound of quick footsteps in the hallway. Then the footsteps paused, and in a moment a voice called, "Where is everybody? Any coffee left? I could use a cup."

"Vinnie!"

The middle-aged woman who came through the doorway into the dining room was peeling off her driving gloves. Her head was bare, and her dark, graying hair was windblown. In the heavy gabardine car coat with its pushed-back hood she seemed shapeless, sturdy, and plain. But her cheeks were as red as those of a child who has been playing in the sun. And her eyes of deep, clear blue were so candid and beautiful they caught the eye of the beholder immediately. It was a lived-in face, strong, vital.

Thomas took her gloves and coat. "Sit here, dear. I'll get you a napkin and some silver." He pulled out a chair for her.

"Have you had any supper?" Amy lifted her face for Vinnie's kiss. "I imagine that's a foolish question."

"Hamburger at the diner, between calls. But their coffee isn't any good. Do I see peach pie?"

Amy poured coffee and served a plate of dessert to her.

"Ummm—good. No one in the world but you and my grandma ever made dried peach pie as good as this." She savored the food.

"You look tired, Vinnie. And we haven't seen you for days. When did we last see her, Tom?"

"When she came for Sunday breakfast and had an emergency call before she got in the door. Two weeks ago, that was."

"That was old Mr. Willoughby's hip. He's doing fine now. His daughter's coming to take him home with her as soon as he can be moved. The children want Gramp home for Christmas, and I'm going to let him go."

"Will things let up a bit, do you think, with the holidays so close?"

"I don't know, Tom. I don't understand why it is, but the nearer Christmas gets the worse life is for a doctor. People seem to confuse me with a social worker or a pastor. I've been called for as many sick hearts today as I have sick bodies."

"Sometimes it's hard to tell the difference," said Tom.

"Why do people have to break up their homes at Christmas? Anytime—for that matter. But why must children have to take it on the chin at Christmas? Why do people who aren't going to stick together ever have children, anyway? I'm getting pretty sick of this casual attitude toward children, especially at Christmas."

"I suppose," said Tom, "if a home is going to break up, the fact that it's Christmas isn't of any special significance. It's the breakup that matters, regardless of when it comes, if there isn't any love to hold things together."

"Why is there such a dearth of that basic commodity?" Vinnie laughed. "Somebody ought to study the economics of love supply and demand. . . ."

There was silence for a moment. Then Vinnie reached out and put a hand on Amy's. "I haven't forgotten what tonight is. I'm so glad you've had love to pull you through."

"It's a hard day," said Amy. "It's just that her birthday's tomorrow—Christmas Eve. We always celebrated it then, you remember."

"That makes it harder, and in a way easier, to ask you what I came to ask you," said Vinnie.

❄ ❄ ❄

There was stillness so deep it could almost be heard in the room. The grandfather clock in the library ticked in its steady, relentless way, giving each second its full and proper place in the passing parade of time. A gust of wind blew a branch against the side of the house with a soft, sweeping sound. The kettle over its low flame in the kitchen snored gently. Each sound was round and whole in the intense stillness of the dining room.

"I've been trying to make up my mind all day to come to you," said Vinnie. "It's about a child. . . ."

Thomas put his fork down, and it clattered sharply on the edge of his plate. "No," he said, his voice coming out harsh and strained. "No, Vinnie, don't try to do us good. We can't stand it. We don't want a child. We don't want anyone here in Carol's place. Carol is dead. No child can take her place. We have forgotten how to be parents. Don't ask us, Vinnie, because we'll have to say no, and it will hurt all of us."

Amy looked first at her husband, then at Vinnie, whose blue eyes were full of love and compassion.

"Vinnie . . . dear Vinnie . . . we know you love us." Amy spoke gently, but her voice was tired and old. "For three long years you've tried all the ways you know to help us. But a child isn't the answer." She put her face in her hands. "Can't you understand this simple thing, Vinnie? When you've lost so much of what your hope and love were built on, there's nothing that can be a substitute."

"Yes," said Vinnie quietly. "I can understand that. It was that very thing that brought me to you. I felt that you two, of all the people I know, would understand that."

"Stop it," said Thomas. "I know what you're trying to do, Vinnie. But Amy and I have come to some kind of equilibrium, and we're not going to have it undone, for anyone or anything."

"Listen to me, you two." Vinnie's voice was warm and very gentle, but there was an insistent quality in it that drew the eyes of the other two to her face. "Just listen a minute, without talking, without resisting me." The urgency in her tone cut through the gentleness.

"I am not conniving in any way to get you involved emotionally with any child. I've always tried to be straightforward with you, and I shall be now. I know—no one better—how you've struggled to accept the fact that one snowy December afternoon, three years ago, your six-year-old child steered her sled into the path of a truck and was killed. Maybe you remember that I was with you that night." She looked from one face to the other.

The faces she looked into were bleak, remembering.

"But maybe you've forgotten something else. For a whole year after Carol's death her friends trooped through this house and yard, using her roller skates, swinging in her swing, playing with her dolls, reading her books. And why?"

The clock struck a deep, mellow tone for the half hour.

"Because you wanted it that way. You wanted to keep that kind of love alive." The blue eyes were very bright. "It was one of the loveliest things I ever knew—one of the most truly beautiful. I'd seen it once before, with a mother and father who'd lost their only son. But the difference is they were able to go on giving to children. What happened to you?"

"Lots of things." Thomas' voice was low. "The children began to forget Carol. New children came into the neighborhood. The house was just a big cookie jar inhabited by two funny people. You know what happened as well as we do."

"So you began to close the door." Vinnie sighed. "Well, I came to ask you to take a child in for a few weeks, as a humane act, to me and to her. There's literally no place for her to go."

"Where are her parents?"

"That's a long story, Tom. She's one of the casualties. She's one of those who are taking it on the chin, not only at Christmas—it's been three years now since she knew any kind of stability, and before that I can guess that there wasn't much love."

Amy refilled Vinnie's cup. There was a stillness on her face, and she did not speak.

"She's been riding around with me all day while I made my calls. It was one notch better than spending the day in the county welfare worker's office, which was the alternative. The worker and I have been trying to find a place for her. No one wants her." Vinnie's voice was bitter. "The family where she was temporarily placed simply refused to keep her another day. They said she ran away whenever they let her out of their sight, and they never knew where she was."

"Did she?" Amy's voice was very quiet. It seemed on the surface disinterested. But Vinnie sensed something indefinable in it.

"Yes, I think she did. She says she wasn't running away. She was just visiting her lady. That's all we can get out of her."

"Her lady . . ." Thomas and Amy said the words together.

"Yes. When we ask her where her lady is she says, 'Sweeping the walk,' or 'In the back yard,' or something that doesn't make sense, to us anyway."

Amy's gaze was locked with Thomas's. But if there was anything unusual in this Vinnie didn't seem to notice.

"She cried once, today—of course it was a rough day, waiting in the car for me, or sitting in the hospital lounge while I made rounds. When I asked her what the trouble was, she said she'd lost her lady. Poor baby. She's been through so much disaster—and now there's not even her make-believe lady to cling to."

"Where is she now, Vinnie?"

Vinnie didn't speak for a moment. Then she took a long breath, which was something like a child's sigh of disappointment. "Asleep on your living-room couch. I carried her in and put her down there. She was exhausted."

The sound at the doorway was very slight, but it drew the attention of all of them.

"Speaking of angels . . ." Vinnie got up and started toward the door.

❄ ❄ ❄

A strange little figure stood there. The car blanket in which she had been wrapped trailed around her. Her tired little face was framed in a blue woolen scarf, knotted under her chin. She looked at the group around the table, her great black eyes masking as best they could her fear and weariness.

She looked from one to the other, the two seated at the table, and Vinnie, standing with her hand on the back of Tom's chair where she had paused, seeing the look on Amy's face.

Then, as though she could not believe what her own eyes beheld, the child stared at Amy. Slowly a look of complete joy and recognition flooded her face.

"My lady, my lady!" she cried, running and stumbling, the heavy blanket still around her, toward Amy.

She would have tripped and fallen had not Tom scooped her up, blanket and all, and put her in Amy's lap.

"We found her," the child called to Vinnie. "We *found* her! She was waiting for me!"

"What goes on here?" Vinnie's amazement was too real for them to doubt that this was a complete surprise to her.

Amy untied the blue scarf. The child sighed and put her head on Amy's breast. With a gentle hand Amy brushed the tangled dark hair back.

"That's a long story, too," she said. "Tom, warm a cup of milk, dear—and then, would you bring me a nightie and a robe, the pink one, from the chest in Carol's room?"

"Yes, darling," said Tom, stopping to lay his face for a moment on her hair. "I know the one you mean."

Vinnie looked at them. Then she picked up the car robe and folded it carefully, matching the edges and smoothing the fold.

Amy was humming to the child, whose lids were drooping.

*There's a song in the air!*
*There's a star in the sky!*

## Katherine Reeves

Katherine Reeves wrote for inspirational magazines in the mid-twentieth century.

Joseph Leininger Wheeler

# BY THE FIREPLACE: A Prose Play in Five Acts

*Dramas come in many sizes, shapes, and locations. Even in Rocky Mountain log cabins.*

## CAST OF CHARACTERS

| | |
|---|---|
| Anthony (Tony) Schuller | *A middle-aged minister from Boston* |
| Carol Lereaux Schuller | *Tony's wife (housewife and writer)* |
| Diane Schuller Graham | *Daughter of Tony and Carol (a TV anchorwoman in Denver)* |
| Barry Graham | *Husband of Diane (an entrepreneur and land developer)* |
| Thomas (Tom) Graham | *Son of Barry and Diane (a junior business major at Vanderbilt University)* |
| Kimberly (Kim) Graham | *Daughter of Barry and Diane (a sophomore liberal arts major at University of Colorado/Boulder)* |
| Cassandra (Cassie) *Graham* | *Daughter of Barry and Diane (a six-and-a-half-year-old first grader)* |
| Lance Graham | *Barry's brother (an advertising copywriter who lives in Florida)* |

## PROLOGUE

"Passengers, this is your captain speaking. You have noticed, I'm sure, the air turbulence. I've just been informed by Denver Air Traffic Control that it is going to get considerably worse before we land, as we are caught between two massive storm fronts: one coming down from Canada and another coming up from

Mexico. Please keep your seat belts fastened for the duration of the flight."

From seats 6B and 6C come these words:

"Tony, I'm worried almost sick!"

"About these storms coming in?"

"Oh no, not that! You're with me, and if God feels it's our time to go, I know we're both ready to meet Him."

"Then what is it, Carol?"

"It's our family: it's falling apart—and it's tearing my heart to pieces. From what Diane said on the phone last night, my gut feeling is that this will be our last Christmas as a united family. You were at the church board meeting until late, so this is the first chance I've had to tell you about it."

"Is it Barry? I know he's made millions as a land developer, and it has changed him. Greed has become the primary motivating force in his life. When he first came into our life he was honest to the core—but I'm very afraid that's no longer true. Several times during recent visits I've heard him stretch the truth or outright lie on the phone. And long ago he ceased going to church. But greed alone would not necessarily doom the marriage."

"You're right there, but last night Diane said, 'Mom, I'm afraid you and Dad won't be happy about this, but there's another woman in Barry's life.' I broke in, 'Serious?' Her answer was 'Serious enough.'"

"But why is she surprised, Carol? There's been another man in *her* life for some time now."

"You mean Mr. Alumbrani, owner of the TV station where she works?"

"Of course! Since the day he first saw her performing in that play at Buell Theater and asked her to interview for a job, he's been after her. Remember, he dumped a longtime anchorwoman to get her."

"I remember. And Diane let him."

"More than that: *encouraged* him."

"I never knew *that.*"

"I didn't tell you, because, because . . . I wasn't proud of what our daughter was becoming. Because of her beauty and charisma, everything she's ever wanted has come her way."

"Come to think of it, you're right: whether it was social vice president, prom queen, or leading role in a play, it has always been hers for the asking."

"Hers even *without* asking."

"True. . . . Tony, somewhere, somehow, we must have failed as her parents."

"I feel the same. Perhaps we should have clipped her wings rather than permitted her to soar."

"Possibly, but I feel the problem is deeper than that. Growing up she was a committed Christian. Somewhere along the way she discarded Christianity. She almost never goes to church anymore. She has always been ambitious, but lately it has become an obsession. Now she's determined to displace one of the network anchorwomen in New York, 'where the action is,' in her own words."

"Mr. Alumbrani is encouraging *that*?"

"Yes, his money enables him to live anywhere. Last night Diane admitted that he suggested that they both file for divorce at the same time so they'd be free to . . . to . . . uh . . ."

"To 'uh' what?"

"Well . . . uh . . . move in together. He doesn't want to be 'tied down' by marriage vows ever again."

"And Diane?"

"She said that though she had not yet agreed to file for divorce, she and Barry have been having serious problems—been arguing with each other a lot. Weren't even sleeping in the same bedroom anymore."

"Doesn't sound good . . . not good at all. So what did you say?"

"What *could* I say? Especially when she added, as kind of an aside, 'Really, Mother, the truth of the matter is that I just don't think marriage is such a big thing anymore. Almost half of my associates and friends are living together without it.'"

"My, how she has changed! Almost wish we hadn't come."

"But that wouldn't change anything. Who knows? Some words of ours may make a difference."

"Not likely, yet, with God 'all things are possible.'"

As the turbulence increases, the plane bucks and shudders, and the nose leaps up, then plunges down or wrenches sideways. The passengers are silent, worrying about their safety. All are quiet, that is, except for two deeply concerned parents:

"But, Carol, what if they *do* break up? Tom and Kim may be able to handle it, but what about little Cassie?"

"A six-and-a-half-year-old going on fourteen. Cassie's *so* adult for her age."

"Wonder how much the disintegrating home has contributed to that?"

"Most likely, a lot! . . . But she's always been wise beyond her years."

"True, no small thanks to her devouring every book in sight. Of course, what else does she have to do when she lets herself into an empty house after school every day?"

"The poor, poor lamb! It just isn't right, Tony! And it isn't even safe! . . . And now *this*."

"But she's not the only child I worry about. Tom has always been the sensitive, philosophical one. A deep thinker. Not athletic at all—just like I was at his age. And Barry has raged at him, shouting, 'No son of mine is going to be a namby-pamby! You get out there on the field and play—like it or not!'"

"I think that deep down, Tommy—can't stop thinking of him as the sweet boy he used to be—still loves the Lord. Those early years of church every Sabbath and church school during the elementary years—they *had* to have left some kind of an imprint on him. Remember, he used to say, 'When I grow up, I want to be a preacher just like Poppy!'"

"I do indeed. And now he's at Vanderbilt. . . ."

"And hating every minute of it. Barry *ordered* him to major in business administration: 'How else are you to take over our family business?' And every time Tom would dare to say, 'But Dad, I don't like business,' the roof caved in on him."

"Poor boy! What a mess life can be. Somehow, Carol, I'm not so sure that the breaking up of his home won't shatter him inside. He's such a sentimentalist—loves family and holidays such as Christmas—*lives* for them, in fact."

"Just like you, Tony. He's just like you."

"Then, perhaps, of the three, Kim may be able to

handle divorce the best. In some ways, she's like you; in some ways like her mother; and in some ways her own self."

"Oh? In what ways?"

"Well, like you and Diane, she's extremely verbal, has a near photographic memory and so is a natural at memorizing poems, readings, short stories, speeches, and dramatic scripts. Like you and Diane, Kim has always turned heads: not just once, but two times, even three."

"But you haven't said how she's different."

"I was coming to that. Like her mother, Kim has found life so easy that everything she ever wanted fell into her lap. Neither of them has ever had to struggle. All three of you attract people like bears to honey—but with a real difference: You genuinely love people; Diane, on the other hand, *uses* people—a huge difference."

"And Kim?"

"I don't really know. I strongly suspect she's more like her mother than you. Only time will tell. . . . Hard to believe that adorable little blonde is now a sophomore at UC Boulder, majoring in—according to her mother—parties and a good time. She's like her mother in that beneath that dazzling smile is an armor thick enough to plate a tank. Both are vulnerable inside, but you'd never know it by the facade. It would take something seismic to crack the veneer."

"It would take a miracle, Tony."

"You're so right: it would take God."

Both are silent for some time, peering down at the skyscrapers of Denver set against a backdrop of the majestic Rockies far below. Finally, Carol takes her husband's hand and makes a request. "Tony, in human terms there appears to be no hope for this marriage. It's such a disaster, you could bank on it. But to God, nothing is impossible. Won't you pray with me now before we face them? Turn over the whole mess to God. Ask Him to use us to fulfill His plan for their lives, for we of ourselves can do nothing—nothing but love them."

So he prays. Every Sabbath he preaches to, and prays for, his congregation, his people; but now he turns closer to home, praying for his children with a new urgency. "Oh Lord, You know that our hearts are breaking, for Diane and Barry have strayed far from You—and almost as far from each other. And Tom and Kim have lost their way as well. Poor Cassie, what will happen to her when her little world collapses? Oh God, we can do nothing to stop it, but *You* can. It would take a miracle . . . but You are the God of miracles—and if it be Your will, we humbly ask for that miracle. In Your hands we leave it."

Opening their eyes, they see the pavilion of the Denver International Airport ahead, seeming straight out of an Arabian desert. The landing rough, they hold hands until the big silver bird, Frontier Flight 636, stabilizes and the engines scream as the captain reverses them. The passengers applaud.

## ACT I

### Scene One

A few hours later, Tony and Carol pull their luggage from the trunk of their rental car and walk along the brick sidewalk to their daughter's front door. It is a log cabin in name only—this castle of a house constructed on a rocky promontory of Conifer Mountain at an elevation of 9,900 feet. Barry built it to endure, to defy any winds up to 200 mph. Baronial because of its massive logs, the home has as its focal point a great room that is anchored by one of the West's most fabled moss rock fireplaces. Four stories high and flanked by soaring glass and steel; the fireplace alone took over a year to be constructed.

Inside this fortress of wood, stone, steel, and glass, on this Christmas Eve Day, are seven people who all walk on eggshells around each other. They test each word before proceeding to the next, afraid that the floor of their lives might give way at any moment.

The meteorologist's weather forecast is grim: "Frankly, folks, I've got bad news for us all. It has been almost a century since two giant storms met in this way. Ordinarily storms from the north move into and out of the Front Range rather quickly, leaving relatively little snow behind. It's the storms from the south that we fear: they can drop heavy amounts of snow on us—but they too usually move through rather quickly. But what we have facing us today is a monster blizzard. The two great storms, both low pressure systems, are expected to meet right here—and then stall out. We predict that this stall will last for perhaps two to three days before moving out, burying those in the foothills and dumping perhaps three feet on Denver. Better hurry down to the grocery store and stock up! This is the long-predicted BIG ONE!"

"I'll believe it when I see it," grouses Tom. "That weather guesser is wrong more than he's right."

Outside, the wind is howling. Diane turns to her

husband. "Barry, would you mind running down to Safeway and the post office? There are some bills that have to be paid by the twenty-seventh."

"Sure. What do you need at Safeway?"

"Well, milk and bread and . . ."

"Don't forget candles," says Kim.

"Do we have enough kerosene for the lamps and the Coleman stove in case the electricity goes out?" asks Tom.

"Yep. Picked that up yesterday. Tom, would you mind bringing in some more firewood?"

"Sure, Dad."

"And Kim, please fill up the inside hot tub and Jacuzzi—and the utility sink too—with water. If the lights go out, the plumbing will stop working and we'll have to flush the toilets with buckets of water."

"Sounds like fun!" chortles Cassie.

SCENE TWO

By 4:15, it is sleeting and the sky is turning dark. At 4:48, from the kitchen window, Cassie shouts, "Look everyone, it's snowing! We're going to have a white Christmas after all!"

The snow intensifies into a whiteout. Tony, standing by the window with his arm around Cassie, predicts, "You know, Cassie, if this keeps up, it'll dump two inches an hour on us."

"That's not much."

"It will be if it keeps up at that rate. That could total four feet in only one day."

"Wow!"

Dominating one corner of the great room is a twelve-foot Christmas tree, resplendent with its lights and rare ornaments. In happier times, family tradition dictated that everyone tromp out into the cold weather in order to find the perfect evergreen. Afterward the tree was decorated with paper or popcorn chains and homemade ornaments. Not so now, for the tree is ordered and delivered by a service that provides the decorations as well. No one in the family has to lift a finger.

At 6:13, the lights go off. Hastily the kerosene lanterns are lit, as well as candles in various candelabra. The lights come back on again at 6:21. At 6:33 they go off again—and stay off.

Gradually, everyone settles down in a chair, recliner, or sofa near the crackling fire in the great fireplace. Kim and Cassie serve everyone a light supper. No one says grace. Tony takes Carol's hand, and they pray silently. Talk drags. Everyone keeps staring out at the storm battering the house.

Tom picks up a phone receiver and announces in a sepulchral voice: "Dead."

It seems strange that even the Christmas tree is dark. And no TV. No radio.

Sensing the awkward silence, Diane attempts to stir up some conversation: "Somehow, it's not the same without Grandpa and Grandma Graham here. First time there's been a break—" she pauses guiltily, thinking of her own discussions about filing for divorce with Mr. Alumbrani, and looks at Barry, who studiously avoids eye contact with her, and sputters, almost whispering—"in our family circle."

Tom almost spits out, "Why did Gramps have to wreck our family by walking out on Grandma and moving in with that woman half his age? . . . How *could* he desert Grandma after all these years?"

"Don't know, Son," answers Barry. "We tried to get Grandma to come alone, but she turned us down."

"What did she say?" queries Kim.

"Oh, something to the effect that—oh! I don't want to repeat what she said."

"Say it!" commands Tom in a strangely different tone than he's ever used to his father before.

"Well, she said . . . uh . . . she said . . . uh. . . that 'The light has gone out of my life—I wish I were dead. Leave me alone—I'd just wreck your Christmas if I came.'"

"And you left her *alone*?" Tom's voice is now that of an accusing district attorney. "You left her there all alone and didn't go after her?" His eyes blazing, the boy checks his next words, fearing he's said too much already.

Barry can only nod, unable to counter the accusation. He can't even justify his failure to fly to his mother's side to himself.

But worse is yet to come.

This time it is Kim, who only uses the term *Mother* when she is angry or deadly serious: "Mother—" and her mother winces—"what about us here in this room, do *we* still have a family?" Tony and Carol shoot meaningful looks at each other: *It's as bad as we feared.*

"Of course!" the words said too quickly, too snappishly, to ring true.

"For how long?"

Silence—deathly silence.

Kim relentlessly bores in, "For *how long* . . . Mother?"

Silence again, then a muffled, "I don't really know, dear."

Tom now looks across at his father and says, "For how long . . . Dad?"

Another long silence followed by, "Well . . . uh . . . I don't know either."

Off in a corner all this time has been the littlest one of all, absolutely silent. She now breaks her long silence with—not a question, but a statement of fact: "And we don't have Jesus anymore either."

Like Tom, Cassie thinks more than she speaks. As time had passed, more and more she missed church, worship, story hour, grace before meals—God.

But she's not yet through. Her parents would be astonished at how analytical her mind is, how their words, tone, body language, and expressions are fed into her inner computers for slow and meditative data processing. Though not old enough yet to be tackling life's toughest problems, she *is* old enough to sense that the great house, impregnable from without, is nevertheless collapsing from within. More than is true of anyone else in the family, each of the shocks administered by her mother and father has increased her inner anguish.

On this Christmas Eve, since her brother and sister have voiced their deepest fears, she decides to clear the air on yet another matter, one that has cast a second cloud, darker even than divorce, over her young life—for it has to do with her self-worth, something never questioned before. She now glances back and forth at both parents, gathering her courage.

"Mommy . . . Daddy . . ."

"What is it, dear?" answers her mother, in her *what-else-could-possibly-happen-to-me?* voice.

"Why didn't you want me?"

Shocked silence.

"I know I wasn't wanted."

Diane gasps out, "That's not true, dear. You were *always* wanted!"

Resolutely, Cassie ploughs on, the weight of the world seemingly on her frail shoulders: "It *is* true. I heard you and Daddy talking about it. You were fighting, and I was scared, cuz you didn't used to fight. . . . You used to *love* each other. . . . Mommy, you said, 'Remember, Barry, we were *through*—we didn't want more children. Then Cassie came along and com–compli–complicated everything. . . . Am I the reason you don't love each other anymore?"

The impossible happens: Diane's drop-dead beautiful face crumbles from within, cracking the protective plates like brittle cast iron. Underneath is raw devastation. She leaps out of her chair and runs blindly from the room. Barry follows.

And outside, the storm rages on.

## ACT II

### Scene One

For a time after the hasty exodus, there is a stunned silence in the room, broken only by a little body hurtling across the room onto her grandmother's lap. And there she weeps convulsively. It seems impossible that a small child could contain such an intensity of suffering. Grandma Carol just keeps holding her tightly in her arms, kissing her, and crooning the tender words that Madonnas and mothers have whispered since time immemorial.

When the torrent of sobbing finally passes, Cassie whispers a question into her grandmother's neck: "And did you and Poppy want me?" Words that Carol barely hears. She answers loudly and ringingly: "Oh yes, *yes*, YES! my darling girl—a thousand times, ten-thousand times, yes! Couldn't even imagine a world without you!" And she holds her even tighter.

Reassured on this all-important question, Cassie relaxes and, about half an hour later, drifts off into sleep.

Only then does Kim get up and sit down next to her grandmother, saying, "Grammy, now that Cassie has had her cry, can I have mine?" And Carol's other arm encircles her, and she leans over to kiss her again and again.

Kim says, "I don't know how, Grammy, I could have survived this night without you and Poppy! You two are the only stability I have left. The only light in my darkness."

"But what about God, my dear?"

"God has deserted me, too."

"God *never* deserts a child of His, dear. Never!"

"Oh, if I could only believe that, Grammy. You have no idea how close I was to the edge—even *before* tonight."

"How is that, Kim?"

"Oh, realizing that home was falling apart, not respecting my parents like I used to—Dad will do *anything* for a buck, and Mother doesn't care who she tramples on to get to the top—then the divorce we all felt coming, and losing God too. . . . Well, I felt life was a cruel joke, not worth living. Oh Grammy, I'm ashamed to tell you this, but I had about decided that I'd just let go when I got back to school."

"Let go?" her grandmother asks apprehensively.

"Yes. Give in to everything. What's the use of being good when nobody else is? Oh Grammy! I'm lost . . . and if I go back to Boulder without answers, I swear I'll just end it all!"

At this last outburst, Tom stands up and beckons his grandfather to follow him into an adjacent room, where candles are burning. There they sit down on a sofa side by side.

The grandfather knows enough to wait. But he doesn't have to wait long: "Hearing their heartbreak—especially Kim's!—just about tears me apart. I had no idea she was that close to breaking!"

"Neither did I, Son."

"I like you calling me 'Son.' I've needed a father for a long time."

"Well, Tom, you *are* my son: when your mother was born, in her basket of eggs were the genetic beginnings of you. Grammy and I contributed those, so in a very real sense, you *are* my son—I've known for a long time that you are more like me than my own daughter is."

"Never thought about *that* before!" says Tom, looking at his grandfather with a new set of lenses. "Now I *know* you'll understand. I've *got* to talk to someone, or like Kim, I'm likely to do something desperate."

"Try me, Tom."

"I will! For starters, I have long felt just like Kim does about Mom and Dad. I don't respect them either. I even find it hard to love them—they are both so self-centered. But in spite of that, they represent the only 'home,' whatever *that* is, the three of us have. Divorce would take the last remnants of stability out of my life. And never again would the three of us have any one place to go home to. God brought you and Grammy here. Without you, on this awful night, this house and all those in it would be going down in flames!"

There is a long silence before he continues.

"Grandpa, I hate—I *hate* business. Always have!"

"But your father insisted on it, didn't he?"

"How did *you* know?"

"We've known about it for a long time. We know a lot of things."

"Even the divorce?"

"Even the divorce—your mother shared that possibility with your grandmother last night."

Tom sighs. "That makes it so much easier—that you know already. . . . I'm *so* glad you're here."

"Yes, we're here," Tony says. "The whole situation looks so impossible. Humanly speaking, the marriage appears doomed."

"Humanly speaking?"

"Yes. Without God. *With* God, miracles are still possible."

"I agree with you there, Grandpa—it would take that. . . ." Then, after a long period of silence, he continues, "Grandpa, I want to share something very personal with you."

"I'd be honored."

"I've started attending church again."

"Praise the Lord!"

"Yes. For a long time now I've been convicted that, without God, life makes no sense whatsoever."

"True indeed."

"And in Nashville I found a church I like. Led by a young pastor who draws in college students by the hundreds. He makes sense and speaks our language. . . . And he's taken an interest in me personally."

"Bless him for that!"

"And . . . I've met a girl."

"At church?"

"Yes. She's part of the group that volunteers at the soup kitchen in downtown Nashville, where all the down-and-outers come."

"What's she like?"

"Like Grandma must have been when she was young."

"That lovely?"

"That lovely."

"Inside too?"

"Yes. And I'm not nearly good enough for her."

"Does she agree with that assumption?"

"Y . . . e . . . s. She insists that I must remain only a friend . . . until . . ."

"Until what?"

"Until I answer Life's Three Eternal Questions. . . ."

"An astute woman indeed."

"Right. She declares that until I have answered them, and develop a purpose for my life, there can be no possible future for us."

"I'd like to meet her. Sounds like a keeper."

"She *is*, believe me."

"So what are you going to do about it?"

"Well, before the roof caved in tonight, I was going to ask you if—if you'd help show me the way."

"And tonight changes things for you?"

"Well, like Kim, the floor of my life has buckled and caved in. Now I'm not in any condition to seriously address those questions. . . . In fact, I'm not even sure I want to go back to church when I return to Nashville. . . . I don't even know if I still believe in God. . . . I'm just—"

"Tom . . . it's been a long and hard day—for *all* of us. Why don't we round up the sleeping bags, and you and I can take turns stoking the fire, as I seriously doubt we'll see your parents before morning."

"I don't know about that. They don't sleep together in the master bedroom anymore, but in separate bedrooms that have no fireplaces in them. Wouldn't be surprised to see them join us later on."

Back in the great room, Kim is still talking to her grandmother. Cassie looks like a sleeping angel painted by Raphael, her favorite teddy bear drawn up next to her cheek.

Tony and his grandson look unseeingly out at the blizzard and listen to the shrieking wind. Clearly, the storm won't be going anywhere else soon.

In time, five sleeping bags are drawn up next to the fireplace.

And . . . about an hour later, true to Tom's prediction, two more.

SCENE TWO

"Poppy! Poppy! Get up! I've got a yardstick. Let's go outside and measure the snow!" calls Cassie.

"Goodness! Is it morning already?"

"Yes! And it's Christmas! We didn't have any Christmas last night!"

*True, and I strongly suspect we won't have much of one today.* "Okay, dear—oh, my back! Wasn't quite the same as our pillow-top mattress back home. But I'll get up."

Shortly afterwards they venture, hand in hand, into what looks like a celestial flour sifter, hundreds of miles across. They are frosted white in only seconds.

"It's *deep*, isn't it, Poppy!"

"Yes, Cassie. Let's see just how deep. Would you believe it! It's twenty-seven inches here . . . it's thirty-two inches here . . . it's twenty-nine inches here. With the sleet that came first, and the wind, and the settling, we've had a good two and a half feet so far—probably thirty inches on the ground now."

"Come! Let's go tell them!"

SCENE THREE

"Mommy, we need to talk," Diane says.

*She hasn't called me that since she was a child!* "Of course, dear. Where?"

"In the sitting room. There's a kerosene heater there."

"Fine."

At breakfast Carol was struck by her daughter's ravaged face. She has seemingly aged several years during the night. Clearly, behind closed doors, something has been happening.

After closing the door, the two women sit down on a sofa.

Then Diane asks her, "Mommy, do you still love me?"

"Of *course*, darling!" And she gathers her into her arms and kisses her again and again. "Of course! How could you ever doubt it?"

Sobbing is all the answer she gets. Not as gut-wrenchingly intense as Cassie's had been, but lasting longer—much longer. It is as though a dam has been breached, and it takes a long time before the lake behind empties itself into the canyon below. When the deluge has finally run its course, Diane lays her head on her mother's lap and silently looks up at her.

The mother tenderly wipes away with her handkerchief the tears that even now continue to roll down her daughter's cheeks.

Then Diane smiles, a smile such as the mother hasn't seen since her daughter's childhood. A pure smile devoid of a mask.

Diane reaches up to touch her mother's still lovely face, then says, "Most likely, I'll never call you 'Mommy' again, but today I need the mother of my childhood. I don't think it's humanly possible to feel more of an absolute failure than I do this morning. I hardly slept a wink all night. Neither did Barry. We just kept listening to the shrieking wind and pelting snow and thinking. We didn't say a word to each other, but along toward dawn he took my hand and kissed it. . . . It has been a *long* time since we've even touched each other."

The mother says nothing, just continues to stroke her daughter's hair.

"Mommy, as the world would have it, Barry and I

had everything. Little did the world know! We had *nothing*. Nothing of any enduring worth. Let me rephrase that: we had *everything*—but didn't know it. We had each other and were in the process of discarding each other as so much trash. We had three wonderful, caring children but weren't aware of it. We had you, but took you for granted, your stability and love for each other, just like we did with Barry's parents. And we had God—and we discarded Him too! Oh, Mommy, how much worse a failure can there be than all this?"

Her mother smiles and says, "I can think of a worse failure."

"What?"

"Not realizing this until it was too late to save all that you now value."

A look of wonder sweeps over Diane's face, restoring some of its lost beauty. "You . . . you . . . don't, don't mean it's not . . . it's not . . . too late, do you?"

"No, dear, this morning, it's not yet too late, but your feet—and Barry's—are on the very edge of an abyss. One more step and you'll regret it for the rest of your life!"

Diane still struggles to comprehend the unexpected miracle. "I can't—I just can't believe that our life isn't over. You're *sure*?" She takes her mother's hands in hers and clenches them with the fierce strength of a drowning swimmer. "You're *sure*? You've talked to them? *All* of them?"

Her mother smiles reassurance. "Last night the two girls needed—desperately needed—a mother. We wept together for hours."

"And Tom?"

"Last night, he needed—just as desperately—a father. And your father filled that role with him. For hours."

"I can't believe it. I just can't believe it! It's just too good to be true. . . . And the children don't hate us?"

Her mother pauses, looks outside at the falling snow, then turns back and says, "No . . . *hate* is not the word. . . . The words I'd substitute are *disillusioned* . . . *disappointed* . . . feeling rejected . . . feeling unloved . . . and feeling unvalued. . . . I hate to say this, but I guess I must if I'm to be honest—they've lost respect for both of you."

Diane sits up, looking her mother straight in the eye. "You've come this far, don't dare stop now! *Please!* . . . Start with me, and that loss of respect—I could handle almost anything but *that*!"

Her mother pauses a long time, searching for the right words. Diane knows better than to try and hurry her.

"Well, dear, first of all because Tom and Kim perceive you as someone who would destroy her closest friend . . . if . . . if such an act would help her achieve career success—get her to the top."

Diane's face crumples once again, just as it did the night before. Again, she buries her head on her mother's shoulder and weeps, saying as she beats a fist vainly on the back of the sofa, "Don't tell me more! *Please* don't tell me any more! . . . But just hold me. Hold me tight. Tell me you still love me!" Again the tears fall like rain.

And again her mother holds her tightly, kisses her, and tells her over and over that she loves her.

Some time later, Diane sits up again and wipes her

eyes. "My, what a big crybaby I am! I've never cried this much in my life!"

"I'm sure of it, dearest."

Diane now turns away and is silent for a long time. Her mother says nothing, just continues to hold her.

Finally, Diane turns her face back toward her mother and says, "That took guts to tell me that—but I needed—desperately needed—to be told. The children are right! I would do just that—in fact, I was planning to do just that! I'm . . . a . . . *despicable* woman!"

Her mother says nothing.

"As for Barry, I can't answer for him, but suffice it to say that we've been two of a kind. *There!* I've said it! 'We've *been*!' I so hope we can reverse the direction of our life."

"With the Lord's help, dear, you can do just that."

"With the Lord's help—that's *it*! How can I get His help when we turned away from Him years ago? Not all at once, but gradually. That has to be the biggest failure of all!"

After a moment, her mother nods her head and says, "You're right, dear, because of that, and the threatened divorce, all three children feel as though the bottom is falling out of their world. I can't speak for Tom, you'll have to ask Dad about that, but Kim was ready last night to give up every principle she's ever valued. She said, with a look of desolation on her face, 'Oh Grammy, what's the use of *anything*? What's the use of being good when nobody else is? If Mom and Dad split up, I just don't see that there's anything left to live for! '"

This time, several minutes pass before either says a word. Then Diane speaks again, but no longer as a child seeking solace from a parent—but as a wife and mother herself. "Mom, how right you are! We are *all* on the brink of absolute ruin. It is so easy to be self-centered—they said that too, didn't they! Never mind, the guilty look in your eyes gives you away. Yes, I've been unbearably self-centered! Never even thinking of the ripple effect of my—of our—actions. . . . I'd ask you what else was said—or implied—about me, but I don't think I could handle it without an absolute collapse. I feel plucked naked, with not a feather to cover my soul!" Another long silence follows.

Then, "Mom, I'm escaping into my bedroom for a while to have it out with myself—and God. I don't even want to talk with Barry yet. By the way, he probably feels like a plucked chicken himself by now. He's been having it out with Dad! . . . Mom, thanks for your toughness. It gives me hope. This morning, I needed to know the worst. Strangely enough, just *knowing* the worst gives me hope, hope that it is not yet too late to salvage our marriage—our home. No, it's got to be more than that! To regain my self-respect and relationship with God."

For a while, Diane seems to forget her mother's presence, and a faraway look comes into her eyes. Almost with a jolt, awareness returns, and with it a new air of resolution. "Would you do me yet another favor, dear Mother?" And she holds the beloved face in her hands and kisses her. "Give me an hour to commune with my soul, then send Barry to me. Meanwhile, would you and Dad mind playing games with the children? . . . None of us is in the mood to celebrate Christmas today, but if Barry is agreeable, we may have an idea as to a substitute activity later today. Bye!" And she is gone, on feet that no longer drag, but fairly fly.

### Scene Four

Some time later, after she has more fully digested the last couple of hours, Carol reenters the great room. Tom, Kim, and Cassie are playing Monopoly. Tony is standing by the window looking out at the falling snow. Softly she crosses the room and puts her hand on Tony's shoulder. He asks, "How did it go?"

Instead of answering, she says, "Come into the sitting room. We need to talk."

Once seated, he asks again, "How did it go?"

"Tough. Mighty tough! But Diane wanted it that way. . . . By the way, I'm curious: did Barry, by any chance, talk to you?"

"He most certainly *did*! Must have been a lot like yours. He led me down to the basement den, lit a fire in the fireplace, sat down in an armchair across from me, looked up, down, and around—everywhere but at me—all the while clenching and unclenching his hands. Finally, he turned to me—and his face was drawn as I had never seen it before. He looked awful! Years older than last night. I don't know what I expected he would say to me—but I most certainly didn't expect what he *did* say.

"He said, 'Dad,' and he choked on that word, 'I'm not even sure you consider me to be your son anymore. . . .'

"I broke in, reached over and took his hand in mine, and said, 'Son, of *course* you're still my son—and I want you to know that no matter what you might ever do or say, we will *always* love you—you will *always* be our son.'"

Tony pauses to regain his composure before going on. "Have you ever seen a strong man break down? Well, he did. Completely. Wept great sobs that shook his body as though he were being battered by that storm outside. I don't think there's anything much harder to take than for one man to watch another man break down emotionally."

Carol reaches over and takes his hand. "I fully understand. Diane wept just as convulsively."

After pausing, Tony continues. "Finally, Barry, after having cried for some time, looked up and said, 'Dad, you must think I'm nothing but a big crybaby, but I have no one to go to but you, now that my father has abandoned both my mother and his children. This new live-in has displaced us all! That's why I came unglued when you assured me that I was still your son—and that you still loved me.'"

Tony reaches into his back pocket for his handkerchief, saying gruffly, "Got something in my eye."

Carol remains silent.

"Well, after he regained his composure again, he continued, 'Dad, this morning I feel as though I was not only a colossal fool—but I was the worst failure a man could be!'"

"Same page of the hymnal as Diane's."

Tony smiles at that. "Well, then he asked me—make that *demanded*!—to be tough with him. 'Dad, I want to know what happened after we left last night. Come now, don't spare me. . . . *Don't spare me!* I *have* to know! If there is any chance in the world for me—for us—I have to know the worst. I need *tough love.*'"

"Again, almost Diane's very words."

"Well, fortunately, you and I debriefed this morning about last night so I was able to respond to his questions as honestly as I could without giving away confidences. When we were through, he was ashen, absolutely ashen. What really got him was the loss of the respect of his children. I'm convinced that this was the first time in his life that he had looked at himself without rose-tinted glasses. It just about annihilated his feelings of self-worth."

"Amazing, how similar your experience was to mine with Diane."

"Also, I *had* to ask him. . . . I looked him straight in the eye and said, 'Barry, how far has it gone with you and the woman you've been seeing?'

"He answered, his face flushed, 'To the very brink, Dad. But, thank God, no further.' Then he was silent for some time—seemed like forever to me—before awareness of where he was came back into his eyes.

"He stood up, pulled me to my feet, gave me a bear hug, and raced out of the room. . . . I haven't seen him since."

"Honey, God appears to be answering our prayer."

"That's what I was thinking. Now we'll just have to see how it plays out."

"Tony, Diane gave me an hour. It's a little over that now. Would you mind looking up Barry and telling him that Diane wants to talk with him in her bedroom?"

"Glad to. . . . This is getting interesting. Feels like I'm in the middle of a play."

"Perhaps we are, Tony. Perhaps we are. . . . And God has written the script."

## ACT III

Scene One

A little after one in the afternoon, the three children mysteriously disappear. One moment, they are playing Chinese Checkers; the next moment they are gone. They do not come back.

About half an hour later, Barry walks over to the two remaining figures by the fire, beckons them with a crooked finger, and they follow him upstairs to Diane's bedroom; he knocks once and leads them in. But it is a totally different Diane than they saw last. Joy has returned to her eyes and youth is flooding back into her cheeks. The same transformation has taken place in Barry.

The children, who have slipped into the room, look at them wonderingly.

Diane and Barry look at each of them, one at a time, then she says, "We have a confession to make." And Barry nods. "We now realize just how close we came to losing each other, losing you, losing God. We—we've been on our knees . . . and . . . uh—" and here her control breaks down.

Barry pulls her closer to him, with a tenderness so long absent in his treatment of her, and says, "What your mother is trying to say is this: We both feel as though we have been complete failures in most everything that really counts in life." And he softly kisses Diane's forehead. "Failures in our marriage, failures in our parenting, failures in our treatment of people in our profession, failures in our relationship with God. How . . . oh how . . . can . . ." and his voice breaks.

"How," Diane comes to his rescue, "how is it possible to fail more than we have?" She wipes her eyes before continuing. "But in spite of that we are hoping—and praying—that each of you children will—will . . ."

"Give us another chance. . . ." adds her husband.

Nothing more can be said, for suddenly, spontaneously, all five of them are in each other's arms, sobbing.

Finally, remembering the other two who have been standing there, hand in hand, taking it all in, the circle is extended to seven.

❄ ❄ ❄

Some time later, Diane turns to her father and says, "Dad, Barry and I have a favor to ask of you. About twenty-three years ago, you married us. Two kids. Well, we never grew up."

"Until last night and this morning," interjects her husband.

Now Diane smiles her impish childhood smile and says, "Dad, we don't feel you've done enough—" She laughs at the look on their faces. "Oh, you dears! Can you be ready, Dad, at 4 p.m., to marry us by the fireplace? The first one didn't take very well."

"Tie us together tighter this time, Dad," adds Barry, kissing Diane again. "I don't want to ever lose this woman again!"

SCENE TWO

It is four o'clock on the dot. The snow is now halfway up the first story of the house. Tony is standing by the fireplace in his suit, his Bible in his hand. Carol is attired in the best dress she brought and is sitting at the nine-foot Steinway. The only light in the room, besides that of the fire and the dim light outside, comes from candelabra.

Carol begins to play some of the same love songs that graced the wedding twenty-three years before.

Softly and slowly, into the room comes an adorable six-year-old flower girl, attired in her best dress, an ethereal light in her eyes, for once without the ubiquitous glasses and pigtails; now her long hair, burnished by brushing to a copperish-gold, flows free and is a thing of beauty to behold. She continually reaches into her basket for flower petals she had taken from her mother's potted geraniums, blooming their hearts out in the south windows of the great room, then scatters them left and right, her grandparents the sole audience.

Next comes Kim, in the dress she wore at a cousin's wedding. Gone is the despair, the despondency; here instead is hope for the future, joy, self-confidence. She makes a detour to the piano in order to engulf her grandmother in a hug, then continues up to her grandfather, to give him one just like it. Then she moves over to Cassie, leans down and kisses her, and takes her hand.

Next comes the groom, attired in a tux. He, too, detours to the piano, then to the flower girl, then to the maid of honor, and last to his father-in-law.

Now, Carol begins the "Wedding March," played by so many, in so many places, millions of times before, but always new.

A vision in white! The same dress—made by her mother—she wore twenty-three years before! Tom found it, by flashlight, deep in the recesses of the attic. He now struts down the aisle in his role as "father of the bride." The piano player stumbles once as the bride embraces her, kissing the mother who did so much to save her and her family. Then the bride detours to the flower girl, who looks with awe at her mother's stunning beauty and whose eyes mist as she takes in the unaccustomed lovelight directed straight at *her.* Then Diane is on to her older daughter, whom she had let down so terribly. Then on to her son, of whom she is so proud! Last of all to her father, waiting with his Bible.

All the while, Barry drinks her in, as though he has never really seen her before. Tenderly, almost adoringly, he watches her every move, reaching down twice for his handkerchief. He now watches as Tom kisses his mother, then he hugs his son before being joined by the bride at the blazing hearth, once again—*it has been so long since he's seen that look in her eyes*—looking at him as though he were all she has ever wanted.

The children—like parched flowers in a spring rain—are restored to life. Each look that passes between the bride and groom is a new crossbar under the floor; each squeeze or embrace another rafter supporting the roof.

❄ ❄ ❄

And now the mother of the bride joins her husband at the front. Has she not been one part of this incredible miracle: God, Tony, and she?

"Dearly Beloved"—all the most moving weddings begin with these two shopworn yet ever-new words.

What is he to say, this father? This father who only twenty-four hours before believed such a sight as this to be the remotest of all probabilities?

"Lord," he now lifts his face upward to his God, "I thank You—*we* thank You—for giving us back our daughter, our son, our *family*. Truly it is a divine miracle, impossible without You. We are humbled that You would stoop down to this tiny planet, one among myriads of Your universes, and single out Barry, Diane, Tom, Kim, and Cassie as recipients of this wondrous gift. And equally to us, Carol and me.

"Cassie—or Cassandra—do you know that each child born creates her own love? When you were born, you didn't dilute, or take away, the love your mother and father had for Tom and Kim, for you are a miracle—there can never be another just like you—because God never creates two of anything exactly alike."

At this, Cassie looks up at her mother and father and says, "Is *that* true? What Poppy says?" Spontaneously the bride and groom interrupt the ceremony by swooping down on their youngest child and enfolding her to them, the bride saying through her tears, "It's true, it's true, darling! I don't know how we could face life without our Cassie!"

It takes a while before the bride stands up and smooths out her dress, now stained with precious tears.

"Cassie, you now know how quickly you can lose everything you love most—if God is turned away from your door. You are only a little girl, yet Jesus would have died just for you, if you were the *only girl in the world.* So you must never, *ever* leave Jesus outside your door. Hold on to His hand, dear Cassie—never let go of it again, no matter how tall you grow—or how much gray sneaks into your hair.

"And now Kim—as priceless as all the diamonds of Kimberly, from whence comes your name. You have learned, my very dear Kim, in recent days, weeks, months, and years how easily love can be lost if it's not continually nurtured. It's like that firecracker red geranium that sings to God all winter there by the window." All turn to look. "How long would it look this joyful, this vibrant, this beautiful, if you watered it only once in a while? Or, worse yet, not at all? Love is just like that—you can *never* take it for granted!

"Kim, the Lord has a very definite plan for your life. And never forget how close you came to losing Him. Remember how you felt: that, without His sustaining power, nothing in life made sense?

"You are old enough, too, Kim, to have learned that beauty, popularity, and status are only temporary. Your face is beautiful now, but it will not long remain so if you do not remain beautiful inside. By that I mean that you must seek always to bring joy into the lives of others. To be always a fountain of God's love that brings Spring with you wherever you go. If you remain that selfless, that giving, you will be just as beautiful as your grandmother when you are her age.

"Tom, Thomas like our Lord's disciple, you opened up your heart to me last night. Quite possibly, those closest to you are unaware of your own journey in recent months. Your own realization that life without God is unthinkable. Your own current crossroads. Your challenge to honestly and earnestly answer Life's Three Eternal Questions. Now that the Lord is being welcomed back to this house and your parents are renewing their love for each other, I am at your service in continuing the discussion we began last night.

"And now we come to the bride and groom, Diane and Barry. What can I possibly say in my frail words that you may perhaps remember in the days and years ahead? That Tom, Kim, and Cassie may remember as well?

"First of all, you have already learned that love must never be taken for granted. One is never 'home free.' In a way, with one's spouse, one must remain on 'company behavior.' When company comes, what do we do? Why, we clean up the house top to bottom, put up fresh towels on the racks, place flowers in vases, set the table with the best china and silverware . . . and so much more. Why don't we do the same for those who are closest to us? Especially to and for our life partner? Always we must show our best side to those we love most. When we fail to do so, love alters, it diminishes.

"Much has been written about passion—and passion is wonderful! But nothing—nothing but God—lasts always. But respect can last, and grow. Always remember that, in marriage, love may precede respect, but it cannot survive the loss of it—*it cannot survive the loss of it.* And once lost, respect can be incredibly difficult to fully regain.

"Remember too that it is the kiss of death to fall in love with the person you married but not fall in love continually with who that person becomes. Barry, you have to be aware that the Diane of today is a radically different creature from the Diane of twenty-three yea ago. Diane, the same is true of Barry. But Barry is going to continue changing; if this marriage is to endure, you and he are going to have to enter into the lifelong adventure of falling in love with all the new creatures your spouse is becoming. Sort of like being married to an archaeologist: the older you get, the more he gets interested in you." The family laughs affectionately at his joke.

"Friends. What would we do without them? God created us to be social creatures who love to interact with others. C. S. Lewis, in that provocative book, *The Four Loves,* postulates that each of our friends unlocks a part of us no one else can ever unlock, just like I said earlier to Cassie. In other words, each friend that dies slams a door on the survivors. That door is now shut forever! The temptation, Diane and Barry, may be to 'protect' your marriage by always staying together, and cutting off your friends. That would be a terrible mistake. For the good Lord did not intend any of us to have a steady diet of any one person: you'd drive that person crazy! We all *need* periodic short separations from each other—'Toots,' your mother and I call them. Without breathing room, we suffocate.

"And love is never possessive: your hand of trust must always remain open. Think of each other as a dove. If your dove flies back to you, it is yours—but the moment you clutch it with your hand, you no longer have a mate, you have a prisoner. Thus trust is the bedrock of marriage.

"In that great book, *Screwtape Letters*, C. S. Lewis warns Christians about those 'long middle years,' the best campaigning weather of all for the Devil. Gail

Sheehy, in her landmark book *Passages*, likens marital life to a diamond-shaped path that splits into two diverging paths that will eventually rejoin each other. When you were first married, Barry and Diane, you were about as alike as you will ever be. But, as the years passed, each of you pursued a separate journey, at a different trajectory. The most dangerous years of all. They are the years representing the widest span of the diamond—otherwise known as the middle-aged crazies. Roughly speaking: thirties to mid-fifties. Incidentally, these are the years when the children begin leaving the home. When the last child leaves home many parents are likely to look at each other across the breakfast table and say, 'Who are *you*?' All too often, parents get so involved with their children that they cease to be lovers. They cease paying much attention to who their spouse is becoming. Too late, they discover they are living with a stranger.

"Only God can keep two people together for a lifetime. Ask God each day to bless the two of you. Praying specifically for each other *will* make a difference. So will wise Christian counselors. Neither a marriage nor a family can flourish unless they draw their inspiration from above. The family that prays together stays together.

"I conclude my part of this ceremony with two great quotations: First, Victor Hugo, in that greatest of all novels, *Les Misérables,* points out that 'The supreme happiness of life is the conviction that we are loved; loved for ourselves—say rather, loved in spite of ourselves.'

"And second, always remember this: *Love reaches its ultimate fulfillment only through God.*"

He stops and turns to his wife.

She smiles and says, "It's now *my* turn. You know, marriage—keeping two people together for a lifetime—can seem ever so daunting. As improbable as—oh—'How do you eat an elephant?' The answer: 'One bite at a time.'

"Over the years we have accumulated a veritable library of articles, books, and quotations dealing with marriage. We have taken upon ourselves the awesome challenge of reducing that library to only twenty maxims. We title them, 'How to Keep a Marriage Together for a Lifetime.'

"And the glue that holds all of them together we label OLEO: Out-Love Each Other.

"Here they are," she says, as she begins to read each one slowly and with emphasis.

1. Cherish each other.
2. Respect each other (and each other's opinions).
3. Listen to (and communicate with) each other.
4. Appreciate each other.
5. Trust each other.
6. Compliment each other.
7. Court each other.
8. Touch, caress, and love each other.
9. Surprise each other.
10. Defend and support each other.
11. Apologize to (and forgive) each other.
12. Be of one voice in raising children.
13. Be there for each other all your life long.

14. Play and laugh with each other.
15. Be generous with each other.
16. Grow with each other.
17. Empathize with each other—and *always* be kind.
18. Journey, travel, and make memories together.
19. Spend less than what is earned.
20. Pray (with and for each other) every day.

She now hands the Twenty Maxims (scripted in her beautiful calligraphy) to the bride and groom, and says, "These are our legacy to you; please post them on your wall where you will see them every day. Each of you memorize them, and recite them together on every anniversary day as your father and I do."

After the vows have been said, the minister/father announces, "It is my privilege and joy, as your father and as a minister of the gospel, to declare once again that you are 'husband and wife.' I now introduce to all of you in this vast audience, Mr. and Mrs. Barry Graham."

Scene Three

It is over. So is the wedding supper prepared on the Coleman kerosene stove. Outside, the storm shows no signs of abating. Over five feet of snow now.

The seven of them watch a sight that never grows old, no matter how many years you've watched it: logs burning in an open fireplace. Each watcher dares to dream again.

All have changed into casual clothes; all except the bride and groom: they merely changed into their honeymoon "traveling" clothes. Diane now leans he head on her husband's broad shoulder. Every once in a while they look at each other like two star-struck teenagers.

Cassie laughs: "Mommy and Daddy are funny—they don't even know we're here." Her mother blushes and snuggles deeper into her husband's arms.

Tom picks up the conversation next. "I like this. . . ."

"Like *what*?" asks Cassie.

"I like having the electricity off, and a storm outside . . . just us here and no telephone—not even a cell phone has rung."

"Perhaps the tower was damaged," suggests his father.

"And no TV," continues Tom. "Reminds me of Glacier National Park last August."

"Oh, wasn't *that* special!" says Kim, remembering. "Bless Uncle Lance for asking us to join him. We haven't vacationed together for a long time—and we used to go *everywhere* together."

"More shame on us that it stopped!" says her mother.

"Tell us about it," asks Grandma Carol. "We got your cards of course. What impressed you most about the park? We've never been there."

"Oh, it was those old lodges—on Lake MacDonald, at East Glacier, Many Glacier, and Waterton Lakes—I liked that best. All built almost a hundred years ago."

"And those funny bathtubs on weird-looking feet—one didn't even have a shower! Had to shampoo on my knees under the tub faucet," says Cassie, reminiscing.

"I liked those antiquey-looking red Jammer buses we ode in through the park. Just think: they were first ıstructed way back in the 1930s!" says Tom.

dreamy look comes over Kim's face. "Grammy,

you would have liked Many Glacier Hotel—isn't that a funny name? Sort of like 'Many Cassie' or 'Many Mother.'" Cassie giggles. "It had a big lobby, with a high ceiling. Out the northern windows was one of the most beautiful lakes—glacier turquoise—that you'll ever see! . . . And in the middle of the lobby was a fire pit with a copper hood, open on all sides. And around it people from all around the world sat and talked. . . ."

"Or played games, crocheted, read, or just relaxed," adds Tom.

"But what impressed me most," continues Kim, "was the people. People who had traveled widely, were cultured, some very wealthy, who talked about the most interesting things! Not like college where everyone is into Hollywood stars, New York celebrities, sports, movies. And too often there's alcohol, drugs, tobacco. One of my sorority sisters—I liked her—drank herself to death at a party. Caused quite a stir! . . . But even that didn't change things. Two weeks later, it was as if nothing had happened."

"I heard about that clear back East. Wasn't it in September?" asks her grandfather.

"Yes, it was. Anyway, it was different at Glacier. Almost like we were in a time warp."

Diane says reminiscently, "What I'll always remember is the Prince of Wales Hotel. Waterton Lakes are beautiful even in the rain. That afternoon tea. The candlelit dinner by the window. And the wind that night! It was worse even than this blizzard. I got up about dawn to open the door to the porch, and would you believe the wind was blowing so hard it was impossible to open the door!"

"You don't say!" responds her father. "What an experience!"

"At East Glacier, they put puzzles together. And people played and sang at the piano. Remember those two cowboy singers? They were funny," chimes in Cassie.

"But those two couldn't hold a candle to that string trio from Slovakia at Many Glacier," declares her father. "It was fascinating to watch the audience in that big lobby. One by one they stood up and gravitated toward the trio who were performing classical, folk, light classical, and old standards. At the end they showered them with tips. Did you see the size of some of those bills?"

"Sure did! There was *money* in that room!" concludes Tom. "By the way, I was intrigued by something Uncle Lance said as we were leaving the park. I thought it was kind of strange coming from an advertising copywriter."

"What was that?" asked Kim.

"Well, he seemed kind of blown away by this peaceful quiet world at Glacier. So different from the world of advertising hype he makes his living in. He put his hand on my shoulder and said, 'Tom, mark my words: you may quite possibly have seen the future in the lodges of Glacier.' I asked him what he meant, and he said, 'Well, we've just about reached the breaking point in terms of electronic intrusion and noise in our life. "Serenity" is almost a lost commodity. God did not create us to be so inundated in ear-battering sound. People are already breaking over it. Just think: the television in average American homes is on seven to nine hours a day, children are playing with PlayStations instead of being outdoors, there's a computer screen in your face all day at the office, telephones, cell phones everywhere you go, even on planes, ships, and vacation spots in the remotest places of the world. Faxes, videos, radio. Barraged by a million ads by the time you're twenty! . . . It just goes on and on and on. So I say it again: "You may have just seen the future." Human behavior can tilt only so far before it changes direction. We've about reached that point.'"

Grandpa had been intently following the dialogue, now he enters the conversation. "So . . . ," he says slowly, "if I'm hearing you right, there was something about the Glacier experience that has been reinforced by this blizzard. Where are you trying to take us?"

For a time there is silence in the room. Surprisingly, it is broken first by Cassie: "Poppy, I don't like TV much anymore. It makes my head ache. And they say bad words all the time. They only say *Jesus* or *Lord* or *God* when they're swearing. . . . It hurts—cuz I *love* Jesus! . . . And they talk like that at school, too."

Her mother, a look on her face Cassie has never seen before, says, "Cassie, come over here to me and Daddy, please."

"Sure, Mommy," and she runs over to them, climbs up, and leans back in her mother's arms.

Diane looks long and searchingly at her husband before she continues. A message flashes between them, and he says, "Go ahead. I'll be with you all the way. I'll rearrange my work schedule."

Diane now looks tenderly into her daughter's eyes and says, "What Daddy's trying to say is that he'll help out—a lot—in our new life."

"What do you mean?" asks Cassie wonderingly.

"What I mean is this," says her mother earnestly. "I've already missed almost seven years of your life—and so has Daddy. We don't want to miss any more! What would you think . . . if I quit my job at the station in order to be a full-time mom?"

The answer is a strangling hug, and a muffled, "Oh Mommy, oh Mommy!"

Then Diane tilts the little face upward and says, "I gather you approve?"

"Oh Mommy, I've prayed—for such an awful long time!—that I wouldn't have to be alone all the time, and that I'd have a mommy and daddy who—who—loved me so much they—they . . ."

The mother interrupts, a catch in her throat. "I understand, darling. I understand," and kisses her. "And there's something else we've talked about today, Daddy and me. Neither of us know yet how to do it, but we're going to *learn*. We're going to be your new teachers. Do you think we'll *do*?"

Now Cassie turns to her father. "Really, truly, you mean it?"

"Yes, Moppet," he says, stroking her hair, "we really do. And it won't be just with books. We're going to explore these mountains together, go to museums, art galleries, all kinds of interesting places. We'll travel—all over the world together. The world is *such* an interesting place."

Cassie is incapable of speech. She just climbs over onto her father's lap, and says, "Hold me, Daddy, and ll me you love me."

Her two siblings disappear and are gone for some time.

When they finally return there is a mischievous glint in their eyes. Kim announces, "We've prepared the honeymoon suite for the bride and groom. There are flowers—geraniums of course!—on the table by the window along with a pitcher of hot tea and a fire burning in the fireplace. You two have been making eyes at each other all evening. It's still snowing, so your honeymoon'll have to be in that room you haven't used for so long. Come now, kiss us all goodnight. You . . ." and her voice breaks, "can never know how Tom and I feel—to—to—see you in love with each other again. . . . It's heaven."

So the bride and groom kiss and embrace each one. Then Barry picks up his bride and carries her upstairs. The last thing those in the great room hear floating down the stairwell is Diane's loving laughter and, "Oh Barry, I feel like Scarlett O'Hara in *Gone with the Wind*," and the sound of a closing door . . . then nothing but the storm.

## ACT IV

SCENE ONE

It is the day after Christmas, and everyone sleeps in. The snow continues to fall. Still, grandfather and grandson take turns keeping the fire going.

Along about 10 a.m., Tom calls out to the sleepers by the fireplace, "Get up you sleepyheads! Grandpa and I have some breakfast for you."

Several hours later, Kim gently knocks on her parents' door. After a sleepy "Come in," she takes in a tray of food and places it on a table near the bed. "Breakfast is served. I'll be back later to retrieve the tray. Leave it on the floor outside the door when you're through." Then, turning back just before reaching the door, she adds roguishly, "No one downstairs wants to see you anytime soon," and shuts the door. She hears muffled laughter behind.

During the long afternoon, Cassie plays dominoes with her grandmother; Kim writes in her journal and in holiday cards to be sent to family and friends; Grandpa and Tom talk softly by the fire. After Cassie drops off to sleep in midafternoon, Kim and her grandmother pick up talking where they'd left off the day before.

About 5:30, Cassie wakes up, yawns, crosses over to the window, and commandeers her grandfather: "Come here, Poppy—see how *deep* it is! I never saw snow *that* deep before!"

He joins her. "Not surprising. Your dad tells me that this is the storm of the century—been almost a hundred years since this much snow fell at one time!"

"How much, Poppy? A *hundred years*? My, that's a long time! . . ."

"Oh, I'd say a little over seven feet—so far."

"I *love* it. It's like a fairyland!"

"That it is, Cas—well, well, well—what do we see? VISITORS . . . coming down the stairs."

"They're not *visitors!* That's Mommy and Daddy!" says Cassie sternly, setting her grandfather straight.

"Well, I'll be!" declares her grandfather, putting on his glasses, "the woman is right. Guess my eyesight isn't what it used to be."

She gives him an indignant schoolmarm look:

"You're making fun of me, Poppy—you knew all the time!"

Barry says, "We're hungry. What's for supper?"

SCENE TWO

Supper over, all resume their various perches by the fire. After a while, Tom gives his grandfather a knowing look, turns to his parents, and says, "I have something to share with you."

His father says, "What is it, Son?"

"Well, Dad, you probably won't like it, but I just *have* to do it."

"Is something wrong, dear?" asks his mother, clearly worried.

"Well, no—and yes, Mom. Let me explain. In recent months, I found God again—or God found me. Found a pastor in Nashville who I like. He's kind of taken me under his wing. But I came home here still undecided. Night before last I was ready to walk out on God again—but yesterday—and Grandpa—changed all that."

"Well, that's *wonderful,* Tom!" says his mother.

"Mom, you haven't heard all of it. Do you remember, way back when I was a child, what I always said I wanted to be when I grew up?"

"Of course! You practically drove us crazy. You were always rounding up your friends and preaching to them."

"Well, I've been thinking . . . and praying . . . a *lot.* And Dad, I hate to let you down, for I know you'd set your heart on my joining you in the business, but I'm even more convinced than when I was a child that Go is calling me to the ministry. Here are the reasons—" He is totally unprepared for his father's reaction.

His father stands up, walks over to him, extends his hand, and says, "I admit that I pushed too hard for you to study business. I've always pictured you continuing the family business." After a pause, Barry adds, "But the ministry is a high calling—quite possibly the highest there is."

His mother joins her husband, saying, "How could *I* say no, growing up with the father I have? We're proud of you." Then the three are in each other's arms.

After they'd returned to their seats, Barry asks his son, "Have you thought much about how you'd make the switch in career plans happen?"

"Yes, Dad. When I get back to Nashville, I'll set up an appointment with an advisor in the religion department. Vanderbilt has a fine divinity school. I believe they'll accept most of my credits.

"Also," Tom says, looking across at his grandfather, "there's something else . . . uh . . . that I might as well share."

"Oh?"

"Well . . . there's a girl."

His mother breaks in, joyfully commanding, "Tell us about her."

"Let's see . . . She's easy on the eyes. . . . She has a sweet disposition, and cares deeply for others—in fact, I first met her at a soup kitchen for the down-and-outers my church runs. Her dad's a court of appeals judge, and her mother's an author of children's books. . . . And I have considerable competition."

"But she likes you best," says Kim, in a *how-could-she-not?* tone.

"Well . . . so far. But she refuses to consider me as anything other than a friend unless . . . uh . . . I answer Life's Three Eternal Questions to her satisfaction."

"What are *they*?" asks Cassie.

"Who am I? . . . Where have I come from? . . . Where am I going?"

Cassie puckers up her brow. "I don't get it. I must be awful dumb. You're Tom. . . . You've come from Mommy and Daddy . . . and you're going back to college—if it ever stops snowing."

Everyone laughs as Tom picks her up and kisses her, saying, "Oh, you little minx—there's just no one like you. . . . Those three questions have to do with 'Do I really have any idea as to what I want to do with my life? Do I look back over my life so far and see how God has led me? And do I have a clear vision of where God is leading me?' I didn't, but Grandpa and I talked for much of the day yesterday, so I do now."

"Will that be enough for the Girl?" asks Cassie.

"Oh you and your one-track mind!" says Tom. "I do hope so."

Silence once more, followed by a soft voice at Grandma's side. "Well, I guess that leaves just me unaccounted for," says Kim. "I've been thinking a lot too, and Grammy's been helping me. . . . I'm—I'm not the same girl I was two days ago. Somehow, I feel as though I've been reborn inside.

"Tom's only a year older than I am—but he's always been lots older than me—inside. He's always known what, deep down, he really wanted to become. I haven't. I'm not even sure now. But I do know one thing—" and here she looks lovingly across the room at her parents, sitting so close to each other there is no space between them—"and it's this: I haven't had parents for a long, long time, and there's so much about life I'd like to learn. I just—I just don't want to grow up yet. I'd like to stay home awhile and help Dad—see if I like land development. I'd like to help with Cassie—see if I like teaching. Grammy has invited me to stay with them awhile. She's going to teach me how to cook, how to sew, how to quilt, and so much more! And I love traveling—I just don't think it's fair for Cassie to travel all over the world and I never get the chance! And somewhere along the way, I want to serve as a student missionary for a year or two. That—I guess that's all for now."

"I'd like that," says wise little Cassie. "I've never had a sister—not really."

"Oh, you will now!" sings Kim, joy bells in her voice as she rushes over to her sister and kisses her.

During all this, Tom's face is a study of conflicting emotions. Now he is heard from again. "*Well*, I like that! I'm the only one who's left out. I'm serious about my calling, but I'm not in a great hurry. After all, like Grandpa told me, today education is lifelong. Grandpa has invited me to come help him in his church and in his revival meetings next summer. But I don't think I can take it if I can't travel some with you guys too!"

"And what about *us*? Are we alone being left out?" asks the patriarch of the family, his eyes twinkling.

"Of course not!" says Diane. "Without you we wouldn't even *be* a family. Whenever your schedule permits, your place is with us. . . . And Tom—of *course* the same goes for you!"

## ACT V

It is December 27, there is eight feet of snow on the ground, and the sun comes out. The white world, especially the snow-flecked trees silhouetted against the deep blue sky of Colorado's high country, dazzles.

All seven stand by the window.

"Let's go sledding!" urges Cassie.

"*How?*" kids Tom. "You'd disappear into that deep snow and we wouldn't find you until next spring—and it'll be some time before we get plowed out."

Suddenly the lights come on.

"Turn 'em off! Turn 'em off! *Please turn 'em off!*" commands Cassie, sounding like there's an emergency.

Everyone rushes to obey, leaving only the lights of the tree on.

"What's the matter, honey?" asks her mother, deeply concerned.

"It's . . . it's just that I don't want things to be like the way they were before—*ever!* I like the quiet, all of us sitting by the fireplace. Can't we keep it this way? *Please?*"

A knowing look passes between her father and mother, then Barry answers, his lips twitching just a little: "I guess that might be arranged, but—" he looks over to the glorious Christmas tree, now ablaze in lights, and the packages, so long neglected—"what about the tree? Do we turn off those lights too?"

Cassie takes a long hard look at the tree, wrinkles up

her brow as though she were being asked to make a great judicial decision, then makes her pronouncement: "Well, per-haps we can leave them on. They're so be-yootiful! . . . *Say!*" as a great light of discovery comes on in her eyes. "Since we can't go sledding, why don't we have Christmas!"

## EPILOGUE

Christmas is over for another year. This time, the presents proved to be the least significant part of the holiday, for the *real* present, the one priceless present, has been the restoration of the family. Of love. Of God.

It has been a *long* day for Cassie, and her eyes begin to glaze over.

"Okay, you dear moppet," says her father, "it's long past your bedtime. Tonight, we all get to sleep in *beds*!"

A calculating look comes into Cassie's eyes. "All right, Daddy, as long as you carry me up the stairs just like you did Mommy!"

"Look what I've *started*!" Her father grins ruefully. "Guess I don't have any choice. First of all, though, kiss everyone goodnight, darling."

The last scene of this memorable Christmas is a sleepy little girl's face, her arms trustingly twined around her father's neck, singing (as she does, her voice slows down, just like a music box winding down):

*With Je-sus in the fam-i-ly,*
*Ha-ppy, ha-ppy home, ha-ppy, ha-ppy home,*
*Ha-ppy, ha-ppy home.*

*With Je-sus in the fam-i-ly,*
*Ha-p-py, ha-p-py h-ome,*
*Ha-p-py, ha-p—*

Her eyes close, and her fingers relax. Cassie is asleep.

# HOW THIS STORY CAME TO BE

Each year's Christmas story comes differently, and rarely does it come easily. Each has its own fuse; some short, some long—this one was long.

For almost a year I had been asking God for another Christmas story, but week after week and month after month passed, and still the story did not come.

I intensified my prayers, each day with a greater sense of urgency, for the final book deadline was drawing nearer every day.

Two trips contributed immeasurably to the story's genesis.

Our son Greg urged us to take a trip with him to Glacier National Park. He had never seen it, and we hadn't seen it in over forty years. Late in August we drove over a thousand miles up to Montana. Having always loved old inns and hotels, we made reservations in three of America's grandest old hotels, the brain-children of James Hill, founder of the Great Northern Railway, and his son, Louis Hill, who assumed the presidency of the railway in 1907. But it was Louis who was obsessed with the dream: build a string of grand hotels and chalets (such as existed in Europe) in order to bring in enough tourists from around the world to make their railroad profitable. In 1911, excited over his dream, Louis temporarily stepped down from the presidency in order to dedicate all of his time to the great project. By 1912, Hill secured a special Act of Congress giving the railroad the right to purchase 160 acres of land on the Blackfoot Indian Reservation just outside the new Glacier National Park.

Now began one of the greatest building feats in American history: the construction of three major hotels (two in the United States and one in Canada), nine chalets, many miles of roads and trails, a telephone system, and a boat system. In addition, Hill masterminded a national advertising campaign combining the concept of "See America First" with a designation of this then most northern of American parks as "the Alps of America." Under Hill's leadership, the Great Northern Railway and the U.S. government entered into a half century of development, embracing both the Age of the Railroad and the Age of the Automobile.

We stayed in all three of Hill's hotels: Glacier Park Lodge, Many Glacier Hotel, and Prince of Wales Hotel. They ended up playing a relatively short but pivotal role (especially as a catalyst) in the story.

The next trip followed two weeks after the Glacier one. During that trip to Oregon and California, my wife, Connie, and I, and my sister Marji and her husband, Elmer, spent two days at Driftwood Shores Resort in Florence, Oregon (see "Christmas Sabbatical," in *Christmas in My Heart 12)*, and another day on the coast, at Gold Beach Inn. During the eight days of this trip, we talked a great deal about the fragility of life, the complexity of all human relationships, separation and divorce, children, the Glacier Park trip, and the Christmas story I had yet to write. Just before we left their home in California, Marji gave me the core plot: "Joe, why don't you write a story about a family of dysfunctional people, including children spoiled by excess, and have the lights go out—just like what happened in that big March storm when your deck partially collapsed?

Then see what a Christmas without electricity might do to such a family."

We returned to Colorado, and as I prayed each day, more and more I was convinced that my sister's suggestion was a "God thing." Finally, in late September, came the moment of truth. *Would such a story jell? Would it work?* As is my habit, I prayed the Prayer of Solomon each day as I wrote, asking the Lord to provide each day's plot and words, that it would be His story, not mine, for only God's wells are deep. I spilled out the basic plot as Marji had sketched it out and waited for God to accept it or reject it. It didn't take long—about a week of marathon days and nights—for it to evolve. It quickly became clear that God wished a significant shift of emphasis: to the effect of separation and divorce on a family and to the role grandparents can have in the preservation of a family. I had included divorce in story plots before, but never before had God specifically helped me to structure ways in which a threatened marriage might be salvaged.

The "storm of the century" that hit Colorado's Front Range this last March provided the setting, and we live high up on Conifer Mountain. During that storm, eight feet of snow fell on us and many homes were without electricity—and I heard many of those stories from friends and neighbors. Our son Greg lives in Lauderdale-By-The-Sea, Florida; thus the destruction and massive power outages of four consecutive Florida hurricanes this fall also seeped into the story as I wrote it.

The characters, I left up to God. I wrestled mightily s I named them, but still had little idea of who they would become. Anthony and Carol are loosely patterned after my minister-father and teacher-mother, with some of Connie and myself mixed in. Barry and Diane change most during the story. Every day, as God and I wrote, they became more three-dimensional. Tom perhaps changes least; Kim significantly more. But, just as was true with seven-year-old Beth in "Evensong," (*Christmas in My Heart 11*), six-year-old Cassie (I tried to change her age several times but was convinced to leave it at six) ran away with the story. I could hardly wait to pick up my Pilot pen each day to find out what she'd do or say next. I wasn't halfway through before I had fallen in love with her. And God waited until the night after I had completed the story to gift me with the epilogue. I awakened out of a dream to hear Cassie singing "Happy, Happy Home." The next morning, God gave me the rest of the scene.

As for fireplaces—I have long considered them to be the very heart of a home.

*For information on the three Glacier National Park lodges, I am indebted to Christine Barnes and her splendid book,* Great Lodges of the West *(Bend, Oregon: W. W. West, 1997).*

*Are you a Joe Wheeler fan? Do you like curling up with a good story? Try these other Joe Wheeler books that will give you that "warm all over" feeling.*

HEART TO HEART STORIES FOR MOMS

This heartwarming collection includes stories about the selfless love of mothers, stepmothers, surrogate mothers, and mentors. Moms in all stages of life will cherish stories that parallel their own, those demonstrating the bond between child, mother, and grandmother. A collection to cherish for years to come.
0-8423-3603-6

CHRISTMAS IN MY HEART
Volume X

*Christmas in My Heart, Volume 10* will bring a tear to your eye and warmth to your heart as you read the story of a lonely little girl who helps a heartbroken mother learn to love again, or the tale of a cynical old shopkeeper who discovers the true meaning of Christmas through the gift of a crippled man. Authors include Pearl S. Buck, Harry Kroll, Margaret Sangster, Jr., and others.
0-8423-5380-1

## Christmas in My Heart

Volume XI

The Christmas season is a time for reflection and peace, a time with family and friends. As you read the story of a father desperately searching for the perfect gift for his little girl, or the account of two brothers who learn a meaningful lesson about God's love from a pair of scrawny Christmas trees, you'll experience anew the joys and meaning of the season.
0-8423-5626-6

## Christmas in My Heart

Volume XII

Open *Christmas in My Heart, Volume 12*, and find hope and joy in the collection of stories—from Arizona senator John McCain's most memorable Christmas among his fellow POWs in a North Vietnamese prison cell, to a warm haven from a Christmas Eve blizzard, to an aged shepherd's eyewitness account of a miracle in Bethlehem. Each selection reminds the reader of the true meaning of Christmas.
0-8423-7126-5

## Christmas in My Heart

Volume XIII

Because the Christmas season too easily becomes a hectic race of *doing*, we often forget to stop and celebrate the greatest gift of all. In *Christmas in My Heart, Volume 13*, enjoy looking over someone else's to-do list; meeting a young boy with a heart for orphans; and watching a soldier yearn for a love that might have been. Stories simply told, but full of wonder.
0-8423-7127-3